TEMPLE OF THE SPIDER GOD

STEVE METCALF

SEVEREDPRESS

TEMPLE OF THE SPIDER GOD

ALSO BY STEVE METCALF

RESET: A Videogame Anecdote
Sketch
The Beast of Trash Island
Objekt 221
Hell Island
Project: REAPER

King Paranormal Investigations Series
Coldwater
Ten Brooks Manor
Paradox Iron

<u>Collections</u>
The Event: The Chicago Rust Yards
The Event: Iron Bay
The Event: Precision Robotics
The Event: Gold Rush
The Event: Wreckage

ONE

Peru. 1853.

The jungle was a blast furnace. Relentless. Overwhelming. Heavy. The air itself seemed to have its own gravity – pressing down against their heads and shoulders. The six miners were happy to get out of what little sun broke through the overhead canopy, only to slowly melt in the stifling heat of the horizontal shaft.

They were assaulted at first by the smell. They couldn't identify it and didn't stop to talk about it. But it was almost tangible. It was a bloated corpse baking in the noon sun. It was a gangrenous leg. It was a half-mauled cow carcass floating in a fetid creek. It was the physical manifestation of sorrow. For some reason, professional curiosity perhaps, the men were undeterred.

It was late afternoon and work had stopped. These six individuals were sent into the mine to examine a potentially dangerous situation. They had evacuated the miners to investigate a crack in Segment 8 of the north stretch of the lower adit – the horizontal shaft cut to drain water, circulate air and provide access to the larger complex. Segment 8 sat just over 300 feet from the outer rim of the mountain. This peak, unnamed on most official maps, was known locally as Little Sister. What had started as a gold excavation during the rush a few years ago had simply opened up as a copper mine.

Valuable enough to keep digging.

Until today.

They worried that the crack signified a shift in pressure that could collapse the tunnel, so a small team went to examine it. The crack was nearly a foot wide and ran the top to bottom span of the path carved into Little Sister. It sat directly in the center between two heavy supports. One of the men, Breer, pulled a piece of the rock out of the right side of the crack. It simply crumbled away expanding the hole in the wall.

"Wouldja lookit that," Breer said, opening his fist and letting the small pebbles run like a waterfall through his open fingers.

The initial reports had called it a crack, but it was much more than that. A foot wide at its narrowest point, they quickly found they had been sent to investigate a tiny doorway. Breer bent forward at the waist and peered through the opening, holding his torch outstretched. It looked like another pathway carved into the mountain running perpendicular to their mine shaft. His light couldn't penetrate too far into the darkness, but he got a sense for what it was and leaned back.

"Some kinda shaft," he said to the other men. "Looks solid. But old."

He shrugged.

It was then that the men caught a stronger sense of the smell. What was once simply an annoyance had now become overwhelming. Once they had the aroma, though, they couldn't get rid of it.

One man, Meyers, stepped directly up to the tiny entrance. He was tall, thin and bald. He had a shock of a beard that exploded from his face. He looked through the hole in the wall and turned sideways. He looked back to the rest of the men.

"No guts, no glory," he said with a smile. And squeezed through the wall into the ancient hallway.

* *

The group of mining engineers was enveloped by the smell.

They were now in something that was somewhere between a cave and a tunnel. Clearly, the path had been touched by workers but it had a roughness to it. The floor and ceiling. Following Meyers's lead, the rest of the small group left the company's horizontal adit and stood on a path that seemed to pull straight into the center of the mountain. The support columns seemed to be created from stone. It was higher and wider than the mine shaft and it ran straight away – perpendicular to the shaft the Angel Island Mining Co. had so far bored into the mountain.

All six men carried heavy torches in addition to the oil-wick lamps attached to their helmets. One by one they started coughing against the increasing smell. Worse, the further they got away from their manufactured shaft, the darker it seemed to get. The men huddled together as they crept deeper into the stench.

Gabe, a broad-shouldered boulder of a man, was in the rear of the group.

"Hol' up," he said. He stopped, mopped his brow and then puked up his lunch. He spat three or four times to clear his mouth, wiped his lips against the material of his left sleeve and then stood back up straight. "Anyone else heatin' up?"

Almost as one, the other five men both nodded and rubbed sweat from their faces. Some men pulled handkerchiefs. Some men armed the sweat away with the sleeves of their jackets. Some men simply ran their palms across their faces. Skin on skin. But it seemed to work to clean off some sweat.

First the smell. Then the heat.

They continued moving forward as they seemed to be approaching a junction. They were more than sixty feet from the crack in the wall. Another twenty feet or so and the sides of the tunnel ended. It looked like it might be a T-junction, but they couldn't really be sure.

"How much further y'all want to walk before we go quits?" Breer asked even as he continued walking.

Gabe, perhaps embarrassed by what he thought might have looked like weakness earlier, shrugged.

"Let's hit this junction and see what we got," he gagged a little, but didn't stop walking, torch held high. "Get a look at the end of this path and we'll head back for a bigger group. More lights."

As a team, they nodded in unison, never breaking step. Finally, they reached the mouth of the tunnel.

"Holy mother of God," said the man they simply called Coop. While speaking, he made the sign of the cross and kissed his closed fist.

The six men stood in a small group, each holding their torches aloft and looking around to cast their helmet lights in all directions. Slowly. It wasn't simply a T-junction. The tunnel spilled out into an enormous open cavern. It couldn't possibly have been man-made, such was the size. There were little punctures of natural light coming in from what must have been the peak of Little Sister. The light filtered through what looked like a blanket of cobwebs near the ceiling of the void. In the center of the cavern was a ziggurat. An enormous pyramidon, perhaps fifty feet high – easily the height of a five-story building. The men stood in awe. A gargantuan stone temple erected inside a hollow mountain. It was an amazing, unbelievable sight.

First the smell. Then the heat. Now the sound.

* *

They should have left right then. In fact, another man, Alfonso, voiced that exact opinion. No one heard him, though.

Everyone had stepped further into the cavern, closer to the huge building. The ziggurat was a wide, blunt pyramid. It seemed to be constructed in steps with the tallest and thickest on the bottom. The layers grew smaller as the structure reached its top, fifty feet above them. The closer they got, they started to make out small details. There was a huge set of doors deeply inset into the center of the base level. There were torches, unlit, all around the edifice, perhaps ten feet apart. On the two extreme edges of the structure were two staircases that seemed to peel up and away from the men. It looked as if they wound back and around, potentially offering a way up to the very top of the temple.

The sixth man, known only as Muds, stepped forward and lit a torch. And then a second one. And a third. All in a row along the front of the temple. It was a thirty-foot stretch from the door to the left corner of the building. Lights flickering, what struck the men was the carvings along the base of the ziggurat. It was like reading a pictogram. The images were of cities, trees, rivers and animals. Snakes and spiders. Birds and crocodiles. They were stunning in their detail.

"Mercy," Gabe said.

Two men had moved to light the three torches on the right. It was then, with all six lights lit along the front of the building-within-a-mountain, that the men heard the sound.

* *

It wasn't apparent at first what it was or where it was coming from. If anything, it was more of a sense. Or sensation. Like the early-warning system that had kept humans out of trouble during their evolutionary path. A rustle in the wind. Grass that moves in an unnatural way. A puff of dust. Rocks falling in the stillness of the night. These are clues that the primitive brain will collect and analyze well before the fight or flight response is triggered.

For these six men, it was a distant series of clicks.

Even though they had no idea what the sound meant, they knew that it wasn't natural and no good would come of it. To a man, they looked at each other and turned toward the mouth of the tunnel they had exited only a few minutes ago. The sound, then, got louder.

Behind them.

They turned as one with their torches held high. It was something out of a nightmare and completely unbelievable. The smell and sound seemed to erupt out of the dark distance and rush toward them. Their minds could scarcely process what they were seeing.

A spider. Of gargantuan proportions

* *

The men froze in a powerful combination of fear and confusion and disbelief. While the spider seemed to tower over them, at full extension, it was only about thirteen feet tall. It was impossible to classify the type of spider – huntsman, black widow – as there were numerous confusing aspects. Each of the eight segmented legs were as thick around as a man's torso and covered in coarse black hair. The two body segments totaled nearly thirty feet in length. Worse, yet, was the head of the beast. A spider's head would be bad enough, but this was the head of a jaguar, gaping maw, jagged teeth. A head topped by a crown of bones.

The huge double-doors at the base of the temple were still closed, so the beast must have come from around the side of the ziggurat. Everyone was rooted to the stone floor of the cavern as if their boots were bolted into the rock. Breer, closest to the giant spider, continued to look into the eyes of the monster and simply screamed. The spider, who had stood virtually motionless in front of the group of men bent forward, crouching its powerful front legs and decapitated the screaming miner.

As if he was a marionette with his strings cut, Breer simply collapsed to the floor of the cave. His right leg twitched, drawing a random pattern in the blood and dirt at their feet. The other five men could hear the sickening crunch as the spider chewed through the cords of muscle, bone and brains that were its prize.

As a unit, the rest of the engineering team turned and ran for the tunnel that connected the ziggurat cavern to the horizontal adit and, ultimately, their freedom. There was a rush of air to their right and the click clack click sound they had originally sensed before the appearance of the great beast. But it was louder and more insistent. Closer. Running.

As it launched forward, the spider seemed to subconsciously avoid the thin shafts of light coming in from the roof of the cavern.

The rhythmic sound was the combination of the bones that made up the spider's crown clunking together and what could have been claws at the end of its legs striking the stone floor eight times each second. Coop, absently, thought to himself, *Do spiders even **have** claws?*

And then he was knocked sideways into two other men – Muds and Gabe – who fell in a heap. The other two men, Alfonso and Meyers, made it to the door only to have the spider lunge in front of them, blocking their escape. Both men recoiled, but Alfonso raised his torch high and waved it back and forth to scare off the monster. For its part, the spider simply stood its ground. It leaned forward and hissed at Alfonso. It was a terrible sound that was somehow both high and low in pitch. Not only did it hurt the two miners' ears, the two men closest, but it also rumbled their chests.

Meyers, absently, reached up to wipe blood that had started running a river of red from his nose down around his lips. He looked at his bloody hand and reached to the thigh holster that held a revolver. Alfonso continued to wave the torch back and forth while taking another three steps backward, toward the ziggurat. The spider reared back only slightly and launched forward with its two right front legs raised. One struck the man in the upper chest and the other struck him in the pelvis. Alfonso was immediately knocked to the ground. The spider pressed down into the man's body and violently twisted the two right legs. With a horrible scream and a sound like a stack of wet paper being torn, the spider simply ripped Alfonso in half. With a violent convulsion, the man died on the dirty floor of the cavern in the center of Little Sister Mountain.

Gabe, Coop and Muds had finally gotten off the ground and they scattered in three different directions. Gabe ran forward to help Meyers. Muds ran backward toward the ziggurat. Coop ran to his right in an attempt to flank the monster. Meyers had finally pulled the sidearm free of his holster and held it aimed at the giant spider. He held the revolver in both hands, but both arms were shaking violently. With the speed of a Gold Rush gunslinger, Meyers fired all six rounds. Most sailed high and to the right, but one shot hit the spider center mass.

The monster staggered slightly to its left and roared both in pain and anger. Meyers kept pulling the trigger, but the weapon was firing dry.

With a bellow that seemed out of place coming from the body of a titanic spider, the beast lunged forward and delivered what could only be described as a headbutt to Meyers who continued to dry fire his revolver until the last moment. The momentum tossed Meyers backward directly into the onrushing Gabe. The two men fell to the hard, dirty floor of the cavern.

Gabe lay on the ground with Meyers directly atop him. They had only a moment or two to crawl to their feet, but they were too stunned to act. Gabe had the air knocked out of him when he fell to the rocky ground. Meyers was dazed by the sheer force of the headbutt. His eyes had just started to clear when he saw the monster standing over him. The crown of bones made a click clack click sound as the spider bent all the way down until it was looking Meyers directly in the eyes. Meyers could smell the beast's breath. It smelled of blood and rotting flesh – a much more concentrated version of the smell that caused Gabe to vomit all over the entrance tunnel.

Suddenly, the spider moved back just a fraction of its body length. It began chewing through Meyers's chest. Through his sternum. Into his ribs. Into his heart.

Meyers screamed in pain, surprise and anguish. Gabe screamed in pure terror. He had not yet gotten his wind back and started kicking his legs as if he was running while lying in a prone position. It would have been comical had he not been covered in blood and the corpse of his dead friend. With a mere shrug of a claw-lined leg, the spider kicked the lifeless form of Meyers to the rocky floor. Gabe, done screaming, suddenly started crying. He held his arms up to guard his face. The spider simply stood on the man's throat – crushing his windpipe before snapping his neck in two.

Coop had frozen in fear. Once up and running, he was going to try to flank the monster and draw his own weapon. In silent horror, he watched the beast kill the two miners. Muds had nearly made it to the double-doors at the base of the ziggurat. Coop turned and ran toward the exit tunnel – the path through which they had entered the temple cavern.

The spider made a snap decision and ran – galloped – toward Muds. It caught up to the man ten feet shy of the ziggurat. It pivoted on its hind four legs and twisted its longer two front legs in a sweeping, circular motion. It struck Muds high up on the back and sent the man flying the remaining distance to the stone temple. The miner struck the solid surface with incredible force. The angle of impact simply folded him in half and broke his back cleanly in two. He was dead before he fell to the ground.

Doing a fast calculation, the jaguar-headed monster realized there was one more trespasser to be dealt with. Again, it ran forward toward the tunnel. Coop had made his way through the tunnel perpendicular to the mine shaft and squeezed his way through the tiny crack in the wall. He was gulping air. His legs felt like jelly. There was an otherworldly ringing in his ears. At least, though, the smell was dissipating.

The spider covered the distance from the ziggurat in mere seconds. It had entered the tunnel just in time to see Coop disappear out the other side. With a roar, the monster galloped down the entrance.

Coop heard the beast crash against the wall that separated the two perpendicular tunnels. He continued to run down the horizontal shaft. He screamed as he ran, with the sunlight at the end of the tunnel representing his finish line.

He never stopped to think whether he could outrun the monster or if getting outside the mountain would truly be his salvation. Coop simply ran. And screamed what little air was in his lungs.

The spider continued to hurl itself against the cracked wall. Each time, pieces of stone rained down and puddled at his feet. Eventually, it could squeeze – not without some pain – its body through the ever-widening crevice. It could have continued to batter the wall to widen the opening, but the spider had a ticking clock in its head to reach the escaping man.

Coop ran.

He had to cover just more than 300 feet to reach the outer rim of the mine shaft. By the time he stole a glance over his left shoulder, he had only twenty more yards to go. The spider was rocketing toward him in a cloud of dust and debris. At a speed that did not seem possible, the monster continued to rush forward.

Ten yards.

Coop would die with a lungful of fresh air. The monster caught him just at the edge of the shaft, sunlight streaming in. The final miner in the group was lifted from the ground and held aloft. The spider had grabbed both Coop's arms and, lifting him up, had grabbed his two legs. Slowly. Excruciatingly. The beast applied force to the man. With a howl, the monster bent forward with his mouth filled with too-many teeth opened as wide as it could go. In the same instant, the spider pulled the man apart at the seams. All four appendages were separated from Coop's trunk. Even before this pain could register, the spider clamped down on his head from behind. And bit down. Hard.

Decapitated.

Chewing on the head like an after-dinner snack, the spider simply watched the torso fall and roll toward the shaft's opening. It took a step forward to grab it, perhaps for a larger meal, and ventured into the direct sunlight that capped the adit. The spider roared in pain as the blazing sunlight blistered across its body and retracted several paces into the horizontal shaft. It howled in anguish at the sun and, after a moment considering its options, retreated back toward the safety and relative darkness of the ziggurat.

* *

Darkness gripped the small mining village of San Pietro like a bloody fist. Two of the men were seeing girls, three of the men were single and one was married. No one had even started to worry yet as the six miners had only been gone for a couple hours. The guess was that they'd finish their examination and come back dirty and sweaty looking for dinner either at home or two of the small town's eating establishments. As the sun gently slid behind Little Sister, darkness enveloped San Pietro. One of the girlfriends had started fixing dinner as had the one wife. The other girlfriend had finished her shift in the mining office and started walking home. The sound nearly knocked her off her feet.

A roar cascaded down the slope of the mountain, ricocheting off the boulders and trees that stood in its path.

The young woman could only look up to the edge of the mine shaft as she heard an ever-growing series of click clack click sounds accompanied by small rockslides. Something was coming toward the village, and she knew it wasn't good.

* *

From the journal of Br. Alistair Munoz, June 22nd, 1853.

We arrived at San Pietro at first light as was the plan. Unfortunately, the town leadership failed to meet us as we expected. We were only two covered wagons and three mules and quickly dismounted to ensure our mission was still welcome.

Fr. Drummond worried aloud that an excessive celebration the night before might have waylaid our greeting and he strode off to find the mayor – or whoever he had originally made contact with. A sudden exclamation, though, shattered my silent reverie.

"Holy Mary," Fr. Drummond shouted.

He had made it about twenty yards away from the wagons down the center of the main street of town. Out of respect, we had stopped just at the outskirts. The rest of our small party rushed to see what was the matter.

It was chaos incarnate. St. Michael and the holy spirit protect me. There was blood everywhere. Doors, shattered. Windows, missing. We all froze, standing in the center of the town's main street. There were bodies all around. No. That's not right. There didn't seem to be any whole bodies. It took me a few moments to steel my nerves and look directly at the carnage but all I could see was a headless torso. Random limbs. Whatever happened here was a violent, catastrophic event.

"We must go," I said, quietly, to the good father's back.

At first he only nodded and then we slowly walked back to the wagons. He paused before getting in, turned to face the village and made the sign of the cross. He closed his eyes and bent forward at the waist. Fr. Drummond's lips moved in a silent prayer. Finished, he turned to me and said:

"There's nothing we can do here."

And we got back into the wagons and swiftly made our way past San Pietro to our next destination.

* *

United States. Present day.

"And they just *left*?" Cal Woods said, perhaps too loudly.

"Ssshhh," came the immediate hush from the other two occupants of this dusty room. They were in a small study alcove on the eleventh floor of the main library in the center of the Ohio State University campus. The William Oxley Thompson Memorial Library, generally referred to by students as simply "the library," enjoyed its status on the campus and throughout the Big Ten conference of schools. Covering more than 300,000 square feet, the library was both a casual hangout and a research haven. Cal was using it for the latter.

Calvin Woods was a doctoral student completing his degree in religious theory. While he had two other classes on his weekly schedule, the bulk of his semester was devoted to independent study. Cal stretched in his chair and brushed his sandy-blonde hair out of his eyes and across his forehead.

He marked the page in Brother Munoz's journal with a loose sheet of paper and pulled his laptop in closer. Cal ran a few searches and finally had to consult his own notes. He smiled as he read his own notes, pulled up the reference volume on the library computer and smiled even more broadly.

"Gotcha," he said under his breath.

Even so, the outburst elicited yet another chorus of shushes from his study-mates. He paid them no heed and packed up his desk. It was time to take this research to the professor.

TWO

Calvin had taken the bus from his off-campus apartment that morning, so he had no bike parked outside the main library. As such, he had to jog across a quarter of the city-size college campus to meet his doctoral mentor, the man who was providing guidance and instruction as the PhD student researched his doctoral thesis. It was shaping up to be a novel-sized paper pitting numerous abandoned religions against each other. Titled "Crusades of the Mind," he was working on the final section of the piece, focusing mostly in South America.

He walked the last block or so slow and carefully made his way through the building. Dr. Emery "Buzz" Crawford had an office on the third floor of Caramouche Hall. While he would have normally taken the stairs, Calvin took a short elevator ride while attempting to slow his breathing. He armed the sweat off his face and tightened the shoulder straps of his blue nylon backpack.

"Whew," he said to no one as the elevator doors opened.

* *

"And we got back into the wagons and swiftly made our way past San Pietro to our next destination."

Calvin finished reading the photocopied page of the journal and Dr. Crawford simply sat with his fingers steepled under his nose. Cal paused for a moment before reaching down to the floor to his over-stuffed backpack. He pulled out a thick volume and hefted it up to the desk. He checked his notes in a battered steno pad and then opened the book to the page he was after.

"Okay," he continued. "So, we've got a mysteriously destroyed mining village in the shadow of a mountain peak. Later in the journal, the missionary mentioned that it was a three-day ride to get to the opposite side of Little Sister."

He fully opened the dusty volume to an ancient map.

"This is a survey dated three years before the journal. 1850. It shows Little Sister right here. And the shadow of what could be the start of a small mining village right here." He put his finger delicately on a small section of the right page of the two-page map. "Angel Island Mining Company was known to mine copper in that area at that time."

Cal paused as his mentor leaned forward and studied the map of Southern Peru. The doctoral student held his finger on the trailing edge of the mountain range for just a moment longer and then pulled his hand away entirely. He reached down into his backpack yet again and fished out another, smaller book.

Dr. Crawford pulled the volume closer so he could get a better look at the map. He nodded.

"Okay," he said. "I'm sorry, Calvin, I'm not seeing the connection here."

The doctoral advisor leaned back in his chair, the furniture groaning under his bulk. The man was in his late forties and was both tall and thick. In a practiced move, he ran his right hand across his chin and through the thick gray-and-black beard that served as an opposite number to his gleaming bald head.

"Right," Cal said, smiling. He finally selected the right book and lifted it back up to the professor's desk. "I read this a year ago and had nearly forgotten about it. Reading Brother Munoz's account reminded me. Something about the positioning of it."

The book was a leather-bound volume, cracked and weather-beaten. It had a bit of twine holding it closed. Calvin started unwrapping it while he began speaking.

"While the Moche civilization largely stayed in parts of the northern coast of ancient Peru, there are legends of them venturing south. During the height of their power in the first thousand years CE, they had sent hundreds, maybe thousands of devoted followers south to both explore and indoctrinate. The reasons for this are varied … but likely tied to the fact that the Moche were not a unified voice. You see, the religion and civilization was largely an amalgamation of others. A confederation of smaller groups. They were splintered into numerous groups all believing in the same deities, but also all battling for supremacy. Thus, there was an internal need to continue growing. Expanding."

"Okay," Buzz said, leaning back from the map, eyeing the ancient text.

Calvin continued:

"One particular group, a powerful sect, had reached the southern edge of the Andes. Legend told a tale of them finding a single peak with an enormous cavern … very nearly a hollow mountain. This peak was lost to antiquity. Never located, but it is said the Moche explorers spent decades exploring the caverns, and building temples to their chief deities – Al Paec, the sky god and Si, the moon goddess."

"Building temples *inside* the mountain?" Buzz asked.

Calvin shrugged.

"The language is unclear," he said, turning the open book around so the professor could see exactly what Cal had been looking at. "But they certainly could have been constructing temples inside the mountain peak. A giant cavern."

Buzz wanted to remain quiet and let his mentee reach whatever conclusion he was ramping toward, but he stole a quick glance at the clock. He had a meeting in ten minutes.

"Interesting, but…"

Calvin smiled.

"There is a legend that states that halfway through the construction of the temple, a group of believers from another civilization ventured into the shadow of the mountain. They were greeted by the Moche warriors and priests together. Open arms. Brother religions. The travelers were offered food, water and rest. They were led down a looping path into a hidden entrance on the east side of the mountain. It is described in the native language as a cave of caves. For three days, and then three days more, there were almost hourly cries of anguish that spilled out of the mountain. It was noted that the sound was so terrifying, a particular type of bird flew away never to return. The travelers, likewise, were never seen again."

Calvin paused, and wiped the last bit of sweat from his forehead, the smile never leaving his face.

"While great chunks of the Mochica language, also called Muchik, are lost, we do know they called this particular peak Pac-Falness. A common translation is Second Child, but there is linguistic evidence that this could also be translated as Little Sister. I believe, these two tales – the decimated mining village and the tortured travelers more than a millennium before – happen at the same place. A southern peak in the Andes. Little Sister Mountain."

* *

The next few months passed as if they were trapped in a quagmire for several students and university professors. Painful though it was, it was not uncommon in the world of administrative academics and international policy. Ultimately, it was decided that the university would sponsor an expedition of six people to South America during the coming summer. Three doctoral candidates and their mentors would visit Little Sister in Southern Peru for 60 days. The student/mentor combinations covered three fields of study – religious theory, archaeology and South American history.

As itineraries were being developed, school administration found it necessary to alert the U.S. embassy in Lima. The ambassador brought the information up during a dinner with a foreign dignitary. This dignitary later told her cousin in the local mayor's office about the student expedition. During a weekly card game, the cousin in the mayor's office told his friend on the security force. The friend on the security force alerted his boss.

"A student expedition, you say?" Dario, the boss, leaned back in the small wooden desk chair situated in the corner of the room. Even though Dario was a small man, the old wood creaked and the springs groaned. "To the middle of nowhere? The jungle? A mountain?"

Edmundo, the man who had just brought his boss the information, nodded. He was nervous, standing just inside the door. He was glad when one of the two oscillating fans caught him with a breeze. Even so, he had to occasionally mop the sweat from his brow and the back of his neck.

"Bullshit," Dario said. "There's something going on here."

He paused, smiling, leaning forward again in the chair. The chair squeaked and groaned in reverse.

"Maybe something dangerous. Maybe some gold. Maybe some artifacts. Maybe these American students need some escorts." He stood up and screwed the cap on top of his sweaty head. "And if they should find something valuable, the escorts can ensure it makes it to the rightful owners."

The two men smiled at the thought. One, perhaps, more than the other.

"Dismissed, Edmundo. And thank you. I need to make a phone call."

**

Finally, the paperwork had all been completed. There were three students from three different graduate departments: Cal Woods from religious theory, Annika Popov from archaeology, and Jenny Renard from South American history. And their advisors: Buzz Crawford, Remy Hart and Gus Del Campo, respectively. They would take two months at the end of summer and beginning of the following school year to visit Southern Peru and study Little Sister, looking for evidence of an ancient civilization. A ruined city. A hollow mountain. A construction project mentioned nowhere in antiquity. A temple lost to time.

THREE

They were packed into a smaller transit airplane for the final leg of the journey from Lima to a small airfield at the southern tip of Peru. This leg would only take a couple hours, but it was a nightmare through and through. The plane shuddered violently upon takeoff and didn't stop shaking the entire way. Locals seemed used to the rough trip, but the dozen or so long-distance travelers were horrified. This included the three students and their three advisors.

There were thirty-four seated passengers and two flight attendants. Many passengers had started drinking heavily to help them pass the time. Either that, or the alcohol would knock them out for an hour or two. For his part, Cal took a couple prescription-strength sleeping pills and knocked them back with a slug of vodka. Not something you'd see advertised on a commercial, but he wasn't a fan of air travel in the first place.

He fell into a deep, troubled sleep.

**

It was barely a town at all. As the mine got bigger, people would have eventually started to move in. Businesses would crop up out of necessity. Hotels. Saloons. Doctors. General stores. They were the immediate necessities. But then barbers. Tailors. Restaurants. Finery. As the population increases, more money flows through the town. It grows. It booms.

San Pietro had only just started picking up any steam and was nowhere near a mining boomtown. The population wasn't even close to one hundred people, yet, and they were all terrified.

Sampaguita, the wife of one of the six miners sent on the expedition into the Little Sister adit, had finished preparing dinner in their small home. Not all the men were accompanied by wives, but as a senior man, Breer had insisted upon it. Now, she stood rooted to the floor staring out the window as the sun finally dipped behind the peak and the village was blanketed by long, menacing shadows.

Then the roar.

Then the clacking sound.

Followed by a small avalanche of rocks, small pebbles and debris sliding down the slope that separated the edge of the mountain range from San Pietro.

Sampaguita walked slowly to the front door of the small home. It was some instinct that made her reach over and turn down the flame of the hurricane lamp at the edge of the table – and again near the door.

There was a scream from outside. She couldn't tell who it was, or where the scream was coming from but she froze in her tracks. Her right hand was outstretched toward the door latch and her left hand had bunched the fabric of her dress at her hip. She wore no shoes and her long, dark hair was pulled back in a light blue tie that matched her dress. Another scream. A crash. The disjointed sounds of people running. Yelling.

She completely extinguished the flame and reached back toward the door latch.

**

It had rained briefly early in the afternoon, but the tropical climate quickly absorbed the water and used it to fuel humidity. Even with the sun down, the air felt heavy and was thick with a sweet, earthy smell. Sampaguita slowly emerged from her home and closed the door behind her. While the jungle clearing allowed some light from the moon and stars to illuminate San Pietro, the shadows caused by the dozen or so buildings of the small village resulted in much of the ground to be bathed in inky blackness. She crept along the shadow of her own home, right cheek pressed to the wall, both hands sliding along the rough exterior – fingers splayed for balance and some subconscious level of comfort.

She was six feet from the corner of her home when an inhuman shriek caused her to freeze in her tracks. The scream was cut short, punctuated by a horrible crunching sound, followed by a loud thump. Sampaguita could hear more sounds. This time a muffled click-clack sound. Another series of screams in the distance. Running, but somehow much less of it.

Finally, she approached the corner of the house and looked around it.

The first thing she saw was the light licking across the side of the building directly to her left. Parts of the home across the street were aflame. While much of the home was crafted using twice-fired clay bricks, certain dried elements such as grass blinds and the thatch roof could catch fire. Right now, the blinds of the home were on fire with the flames gently stretching toward the roof.

This gave Sampaguita pause as it was so uncommon. Her silent reverie was shattered by a scream that echoed across the length of the village. The terrible sound was followed by another crunch and punctuated by what could have been a door splintering.

She took a tentative step around the corner of the building and her naked foot was suddenly wet and cold. Sampaguita looked down only to see the light of the fire illuminating a puddle of dark liquid. Further into the shadows, though, was a destroyed body. She could tell that the body was male, but that was all she could deduce. The legs were pulled apart at a savage angle, the chest was caved in and punctured. Worst, though, was that the corpse was decapitated. The head was nowhere to be seen.

Immediately, both hands went to cover her mouth and stifle a scream. She jerked to her left to step out of the puddle of blood. For the moment, the mining village of San Pietro was quiet. She could only hear the gentle crackle of fire that had now spread to begin engulfing the roof of the hut directly in front of her.

Click clack click.

She crept around the corner of the next building and turned to face the main thoroughfare through the three-dozen buildings that comprised San Pietro. To her right, the main street led to the gentle curve of the river. To her left, she could see the peak of Little Sister as the moon peeked around the north face.

Part of the burning roof caved in and, startled, Sampaguita turned to face the sound. Something else caught her attention, though, as her field of vision rapidly shifted from the left to the right. A body, gasping for breath. She ran and crouched next to the person. It was a man. Cesar Haro. A miner. He lay in the dirt, against the wall of his own home, unmoving save for the uncontrollable twitching of his extremities. The heels of his feet drummed a disjointed pattern against the mud captured against the building. He looked at her as he sucked increasingly desperate breaths. Eyes wide. Terrified of what he had seen – of what lay ahead.

He let his gaze shift to the right, looking around Sampaguita's left hip. His eyes widened and he struggled to suck down a lungful of air. Twice. Three times. And then he stopped breathing. Eyes wide in fear.

Quietly sobbing, Sampaguita made the sign of the cross and then froze. What had Cesar seen?

Slowly, she turned in her crouch. She didn't dare make a sound or stand up. The hairs along both forearms stood ramrod straight. She squinted her eyes and steeled her nerves as best she could. As she turned, there was Little Sister, now wearing the moon as a halo.

Click clack click.

Illuminated by fire at the end of the street – behind her – she could barely make out a sight that defied explanation. A spider as tall as a building. It had the head of a jaguar, mouth opened in a silent roar. It started to rush toward her and she could see that the clacking sound was the result of a crown of bones – large human leg bones – draped around its horrible head.

She opened her mouth to scream –

**

Calvin jerked awake with a start. He was still on the small transit airplane, but, for a strange moment, he was in both places. At once, he was 30,000 feet in the air and struggling for his life in a terror-torn mining camp in Southern Peru. Gradually, he came to his senses and rubbed his eyes with the palms of both hands.

"Bad dream?"

He looked to his right. Occupying the seat next to him was another student – Jenny Renard – from the South American History department. Jenny was the youngest in the group and, coincidentally, the smallest. She wore her large personality draped across a petite frame. Her hair was a short bob and she pushed some strands behind her right ear and adjusted her glasses with her right hand at nearly the same time – a practiced, almost nervous move.

"Yeah, I guess," Calvin said. "Why do you ask?"

Jenny shrugged.

"You were moaning and, like, spasmed or something when you were waking up," she said, turning back to her book.

Calvin sent her his own shrug in response.

"I'm kinda losing it already," he said. "But I think I was dreaming about the mining village. San Pietro. What the missionaries must have seen to get them to run away so quickly. There was a fire."

He paused for a moment, trying to recapture the spirit of the nightmare. Finally, Cal shook his head and frowned.

"Nope," he said turning to Jenny. "It's gone."

She nodded her head in understanding.

"Yeah. Mine are like that, too. Once I wake up … gone. Just evaporated."

Jenny took a small package of crackers out of her backpack and offered the snack to Calvin. He shook his head as a pocket of turbulence sent a jolt of violence through the small plane.

"Thanks," he said. "I should probably just wait until we're on the ground."

She smiled, shrugged, and popped a few of the cheese-flavored crackers into her mouth, grinning and chewing away while plugging her ear buds back in.

**

Safely on the ground, the six academics collected their gear and walked into the small airport. They waited for their luggage to be removed from the belly of the transit plane so they could leave. The plan was to stay at a local hotel for one evening and head out after getting a good night's rest.

As the six explorers stood in a small group, they were approached by four men wearing combat fatigues. The lead man walked directly up to Dr. Crawford and extended his hand.

"Dario Escalante, Mayoral Security Force," he said, both shaking the professor's hand and snapping off a smart nod. Not letting go of the elder man's hand, he nodded over his right shoulder at the other three men. "Edmundo. Ramon. Javier."

The three men were dressed similarly to Dario and seemed interchangeable. That is, except for Javier, who looked like a tank of a man. Several inches taller than the others and several pounds thicker, the man's outfit stretched across his chest as he stood with his hands clasped behind his back. None of the men smiled or even indicated the presence of the American college students.

Crawford released Dario's hand.

"Dr. Emery Crawford," he said. "I wasn't aware we were receiving a military greeting."

Dario grinned.

"Well, señor, this is not the whole of the situation," the security man said. He spoke with ease in the second language, but with a heavy accent. "Many people, how you say, raised a red flag." He paused to smile.

The professor's face remained largely impassive, but what was left of his smile finally faltered.

"I don't understand," he said.

The security lead shrugged, the smile never leaving his face.

"This jungle is dangerous, no? And your group is from the school," Dario said. "You will be in the jungle. Looking for the secret mountain." His smile grew by several degrees. "We will accompany you and keep you safe. Protect you." He waved briefly to the three men behind him, and turned back to the professor. "Welcome to Peru, señor. Mañana, then. Sleep well."

**

"Unacceptable," Gus Del Campo said.

They had rented two rooms in a local hotel – one for the three female academics and one for the three males. It was mid-afternoon and everyone was trying to relax from the long flight and the strange encounter at the airport. The three advisors had congregated in the male room while the students were lounging in the female room.

Ignatius "Gus" Del Campo was a professor of South American History and the most tenured member of the group. With a wild shock of gray hair and dark features, he looked both manicured and out of control at the same time. Usually, the clue was the look in his eyes. Right now, his eyes were wild.

"And now we have a military escort for an academic exploration?" Del Campo asked the room in general. Dr. Crawford shrugged. He was resting in a small, fabric-upholstered armchair in the far corner of the room near an oscillating fan that had seen better days.

The third, Remy Hart, professor of archaeology, sat on the edge of one of the small beds. She had grown up in an equatorial climate, so the Peru heat was nothing new to her. She wore shorts and an athletic-cut t-shirt. Her medium-length black hair was pulled back into a tight ponytail. She looked back and forth from the two men, a frown on her face.

"It's not an escort, Gus," she said, and paused for a moment. "They don't trust us. It's a babysitting detail."

"They said they were in place to keep us safe," Crawford said from his chair. He started fanning himself with a magazine.

Remy shook her head.

"Sure, they're going to say that. What else *can* they say?"

"They think we're going to destroy priceless artifacts? Ruin their cultural heritage?" Gus said. He had stopped pacing and was looking at Dr. Hart, thinking.

Again, she shook her head.

"Maybe," she said. "But I don't think so." She was pensive, pinching her lower lip between the thumb and index finger of her right hand – a habit developed decades ago during intense study sessions. "It's almost like …"

"Greed," Crawford said.

"They are worried we're going to find some ancient gold, gems, artwork," Hart nodded, and then shrugged. "I don't know what they think. But I think it's pretty clear that they were ordered to accompany us to make sure we didn't find and remove anything of value."

"That has nothing to do with our stated goal," Del Campo said, again pacing the small room. They could hear laughter from the student room. Gus looked at the wall, a scowl carved across his forehead. "We're here to uncover a mysterious temple. Heretofore unrealized. Buried in two wholly unrelated texts …"

"Potentially filled with gold," Crawford said, nodding at Hart. "She's right. It doesn't matter what our stated goal is. The officials in this region are hyper-sensitive to tourists removing priceless antiques. Believe me, getting through customs will be much harder leaving the country than it was getting in."

The room was silent for a moment. They heard the clunk of the oscillating fan as it hit its extreme left side, reset, and moved right again. And then the laughter from the room full of students.

"What do we do?" Remy finally broke the silence.

Gus sat on the other twin bed, facing his two companions. He said nothing, just folded his hands between his knees.

"Nothing," Crawford said, and shrugged. "We have to assume they mean us no harm. If they're truly here to keep us out of trouble and lighten our loads if we do happen to find anything … more power to them. These aren't the '40s. Or even the '80s. We're never truly alone. We can livestream or, at the very least, record and transmit data at any time. They have to know that. There might not be cell towers in the middle of the jungle, but we still have options."

Dr. Hart nodded.

"I'll put Annika on it," she said. Annika Popov was her doctoral student. A U.S. born Russian, she was a tech-wiz and often ran the professor's presentations at national conventions.

Dr. Crawford nodded in response.

"Okay," he said. "That'll be some kind of backup. I suppose we can record some kind of hokey *Here we are starting our adventure* clip tomorrow and make sure to get our military escort's faces clearly in frame. That should get the point across without really spelling it out."

"Done," Hart said. She stood up off the bed. "What do you say? Early dinner? Early to bed?"

The two men stood as well, nodding.

"A river cuts through rock, not because of its power, but because of its persistence," Professor Del Campo said, heading for the door.

**

The room next door was largely the same as the one currently occupied by the three professors. This one, designated as the 'female room' because the lady academics – two students and Professor Hart – would sleep here this evening. With any luck, they'd be back in these same rooms in a few days after exploring the mystery of Little Sister Mountain.

There were two twin beds made up and a cot stood up in the corner of the room. There was a sitting chair with a small table next to it. There was no AC control unit, but a medium-sized oscillating fan occupying the opposite corner of the room from the chair. Cal Woods sat in the chair and the two ladies each sat on a bed.

Jenny Renard, who had witnessed Cal's difficulty waking up from a nightmare on the airplane, and Annika Popov couldn't be more different in terms of background or physicality. Annika was tall, thin and muscular with long blonde hair. She had modeled for magazine ads and clothing catalogs as a youth but lost interest in it when it threatened to take over her life. While a cute kid, puberty had turned her into the stereotypical Russian beauty. Even in her mid-teens, she realized that she didn't want to chase that profession and turned toward academia. Her grandparents on her mother's side had immigrated to the United States in the '60s. Annika's mother married a young man in college – on a student visa from Russia – and became pregnant soon after.

"Seriously?" Annika said and laughed. She had a slight Russian accent from her access to her community and the language her extended family spoke at gatherings. Plus, every few years, she took a long visit to her ancestral homeland over the school summer vacation.

Cal, a boy who barely ventured out of the Midwest, found her accent exotic. He almost had a constant smile on his face when they hung out. He lacked the courage to ask her out, but was also bad at keeping secrets. Or masking his emotions.

"Really," he said, leaning back in the chair and laughing. Jenny was laughing so hard she had to wipe tears from her eyes. She was sitting on one bed propped up with pillows, her back leaning against the wall. Annika was sitting cross-legged at the foot of the other bed.

"So, here I am," Cal continued. "Summer retail job. Big department store in my hometown. This old lady is trying to return some sort of portable griddle. It's used. Clearly. Still warm from her cooking some pancakes for breakfast that morning."

"Still warm," Jenny said, snorting.

"Yeah," Cal laughed. "She had no receipt. I don't think we had even carried that thing in the store for a couple years. I told her that we couldn't return it like she wanted to. She lost it. *This is the worst day of my life,* she screamed."

"Lucky her," Annika said.

"Right? That's exactly what my buddy Felix said later. Her not scamming us out of fifty bucks was the worst thing that ever happened to her? A broken griddle is the worst thing that ever happened to her? That's pretty awesome. Anyway, my manager comes over because she hears the commotion, and the old lady lays out her case. Manager goes, *So did you bring us any pancakes?*"

Another peel of laughter from the students.

"I'm sure she wasn't happy about that," Annika said.

"Nah," Calvin said, shaking his head. "She bundled up the griddle and stormed out of there. It was hysterical."

Annika picked up her phone and typed out a note to herself to use later. When she got to the end of the note, she read aloud as she typed.

"Hashtag Worst Day Ever," she said and laughed again. She slid the phone back into the hip pocket of her yoga pants. The phone was a fresh piece of technology, but had a battered, pink case with a butterfly sticker on the back. The story was it was a gift from a long-dead relative and she had to pay to have it custom-fitted to whatever new phone came out.

Soon there was a knock at the door signaling it was time for dinner.

FOUR

First thing in the morning means something different across ages and occupations. It is an inaccurate measure for both students and professors. Fortunately, the latter had communicated their understanding to the former well in advance. At first light, all three students – Calvin, Annika, Jenny – and all three professors – Crawford, Hart, Del Campo – met in the hotel lobby ready to officially begin their Peruvian adventure. They had arranged transportation far past the city's outskirts and into the jungle. They had planned to hike through the jungle with a local guide and come back at a pre-determined time. They had packed enough provisions for a week in the jungle and would come back to the hotel to rest and compare notes.

According to official documentation, the expedition could last as long as sixty days, but their realistic itinerary was only for half that time. It would take a monumental discovery to keep them longer. In truth, a monumental discovery might actually cut the excursion shorter as they would mark the find with GPS coordinates and wait to align with a larger force to fully explore the ruins. In point of fact, though, most members of the party thought they could find what they needed to find in two weeks and then escape back to the comforts of home. Though they wouldn't admit to it out loud. Whatever happened, it would make for an interesting PhD thesis and, potentially, a published paper.

But, as they say, plans change.

They exited the hotel directly into blinding light and crushing humidity.

"Oof," Calvin said without meaning to.

"Oh dear God," Annika said.

Dr. Del Campo simply smiled and breathed the heavy air deeply into his lungs.

"Good morning, Mr. Equator," he grinned. The smile, unfortunately, evaporated just as quickly as it had appeared.

Standing in the street, traffic moving past them in a strange combination of fear and reverence, were the four members of the mayor's special security force. Dario Escalante was joined by Edmundo, Ramon and the monstrous Javier. Just like yesterday at the airport, the senior man wore a constant, radiant smile. The four men were dressed in military fatigues and wore large backpacks that rivaled the ones carried by the six academics.

"Buenos dias," Dario said, stepping forward. "Good morning, my friends. I trust you slept well. Actually, I am sure you did not. Considering the excitement of our upcoming journey, no? We thought it would be better to dismiss your escort and provide our own convoy."

He gestured toward the three military Jeeps that were parked across the street – pointing down the main road out of San Pietro. The vehicles looked well-used but also well cared-for. Painted a dark green, they waited for the ten-member excursion.

"Now see here," Dr. Crawford stepped forward toward Dario. The military leader and, oddly, Javier did not react, but the other two men stiffened visibly. Annika made no secret that she pulled her phone out of a hip pocket and held it to her face. She started recording the interaction. The way she moved the camera made it clear that she kept Crawford in the frame, but also focused in on the four military men in turn. "We have already made arrangements and, frankly, we don't need your help or your protection. I'll thank you to be on your way."

Dario Escante grinned even wider and paused for a moment. He nodded.

"I understand," he said, putting his hands in his pockets, a calculated non-threatening posture. "I'm sure you find this lack of communication both frustrating and alarming. But the decision was made outside my house. Um, over my head? I think this is your phrase. You are now our guests and we your protectors. You will succeed in your mission, señor. I know this." His grin turned into a full-on smile, and he winked at the six academics as a group.

There was a moment of silence between both groups. Cars continued to pass. Foot traffic on the sidewalk continued to increase in volume. The city was slowly waking up and venturing out into the early morning humidity.

"Come, Professor," Dario said, pulling his right hand out of his pocket, gesturing it again toward the parked convoy. "This subject is beyond debate. You have nothing to fear. Please accept our hospitality. Let us find your hidden temple."

**

It was a hard 160 miles. In what might have been a pleasant trip across many United States highways, the ten-strong team was forced to endure several hours over rough terrain. While the road directly out of San Pietro was pleasant, the path become progressively worse with every turn. Eventually, they were on a winding, single-lane path with little clearance on either side of their Jeeps. Thick branches reached out from the lush jungle and scraped along the sides of the three military vehicles. It was little more than a path fit for walking livestock from ranch to ranch.

The team members all reacted in different ways. For the military men who were local to the area, it was just another drive outside spots with regular traffic and habitation. Some of the academics were watching with rapt attention. Some were reading their notes and making notes on their phones.

Annika was quietly speaking to her phone in a combination of English and Russian. She looked to be recording a podcast. Calvin, however, simply stared straight ahead.

He watched out the front window of the military Jeep and retreated inside his own mind, almost as if he was narrating a chapter of his doctoral thesis.

**

While the argument certainly follows that all buildings are built with a purpose in mind, thoughts immediately turn to dramatic projects. Skyscrapers, shopping malls, sports arenas – these purpose-built structures capture the attention of modern audiences. It has simply become a way of life. Billions of dollars and years of planning and execution go into these village-sized monstrosities. But what of the classic ways? Castles across Europe are thousands of years old. Intricate. Effective. Astonishing. The Citadel of Aleppo contains structures that were crafted more than five thousand years ago, dating back to 3,000 B.C.

Similarly, religious temples dot spots across the Earth with a staggering array of age, purpose and drama.

One such example is Gobekli Tepe. First uncovered and dismissed as a simple medieval grave, archaeologists have been unearthing the temple for the last twenty years. Dating back to 10,000 B.C., it is an astonishing series of structures with chambers, altars, carvings and rooms. Archaeologists now believe that the holy site was used as a gathering place for visitors from many surrounding agrarian societies. It could very well mean the beginning of larger civilization. Right there in southeastern Turkey. A gentle slope with a name that softly translates to "Belly Hill," Gobekli Tepe was rumored to have been the real-life Garden of Eden – the crossroads of modern civilization at the time. While that claim has been disproved as a literal thought, it could very well be more of a figurative understanding.

We should note that the structure was covered over with soil around 8,000 B.C. Researchers have not discovered a reason for the intentional backfill, but it represents a boon for us in the future. The structure was completely buried and protected from the elements for more than ten thousand years.

Which is why the possibility of a structure near Little Sister is so intriguing. If it is a heretofore unfound temple from the Moche or a contemporary civilization, it would represent a career-defining find.

While information is light, there are rumors of a hidden ziggurat that served as a temple to a chief figure of the Mochican belief system. The Moche would offer blood sacrifices to Ai Apaec, the sun god, through his most powerful deity. The God of Darkness. The Decapitator. Even though a fearsome deity, he was seen as sort of a protector. Captured warriors were offered to him as sacrifices often with bloodletting, torture and decapitation.

But the question remains ... what if there were no captured warriors? What if the Decapitator was brought to life in anticipation of battle where none ultimately unfurled? How would the God of Darkness be sated?

Maybe these are the types of questions that could be addressed after uncovering a secret temple buried in the shadow of the peak of Little Sister, hidden in the blood of an eviscerated mining village.

**

"We have arrived," Dario said loudly, broadcasting to the other nine members of the expedition. They had pulled some distance into the jungle off the livestock-path they had used to travel for the last several hours. It was a small clearing, and they parked the three Jeeps side-by side with only enough room to open the doors between them.

The other people all piled out, stretching their legs and backs. Even the military men were cracking their necks to loosen up the tight muscles there. They had worked hard to appear unperturbed, but it was a difficult drive through challenging terrain. It was nice to be off the road.

"It might be wise to take a bathroom break, no?" Dario smiled as he walked past Dr. Crawford and clapped him on the back. "But don't wander too far. These trees often hide a fearsome secret."

The academics all looked at each other.

While waiting for the paperwork to go through, they had been instructed to read as much as they could about the Peruvian jungles. Dangerous flowers. Predators. Poisonous plants. Deadly insects. This was an expedition that balanced on the backs of numerous signed release forms with each student carrying an extensive emergency medical kit that included epi-pens and antivenom.

Annika paused for a moment and, having a thought, pulled out her phone to once again make a recording.

"Here we are in the jungle," she said, her lilting accent causing Calvin to stretch a bit longer than he had originally planned. He had to pee, but it would have to wait. "Peru," Annika continued. "Escorted by our fearless betters in the search for a mysterious hidden temple. Buried for hundreds of years inside a hollow mountain. Little Sister Mountain. The southern tip of the Andes."

She started walking a few paces, but not leaving the shadow of the parked military vehicles. Still talking, she did a slow twirl, making sure to get the faces of all four security force members in the camera's view.

"They are armed with pistols, knives and machetes to ensure we reach our destination safely and in one living piece. I have nothing to fear from the jungle … only the vengeful ghost of the Decapitator. The God of Darkness. The Spider

God." With one more twirl, she deactivated the phone for now.

Dario looked at Edmundo, a silent conversation passing between the two men.

**

After only ten minutes of walking, the jungle had swallowed the entire team whole. They had adopted a single-file line with the best guide in the front, and the second-best guide in the back. Javier was second in line, followed by the six tourists and Dario right behind them so he could keep an eye on ninety percent of the group.

"The Amazon River cuts a swath east to west across the top of South America," Annika said, speaking to her phone. She wasn't broadcasting anything, but simply recording a movie to be edited and produced later. He kept moving out of frame, but Annika was careful to get Dario in view as often as possible. "It is surrounded by the Amazon Rainforest that spreads out to the extent that it covers forty percent of South America. Nearly seven million square kilometers. While we are in a jungle in Peru, we're more to the south. A jungle, but not THE jungle."

She took a few steps in silence, looking around at her surroundings, sliding the camera view around to take in the trees and sunlight streaming through the leafy canopy.

"I'm swathed nearly head to toe in LYCRA spandex and canvas with only my hands and face uncovered," she was not exaggerating for effect. Even in the sweltering heat and humidity, everyone wore clothing limiting the exposed skin to protect it from insect bites and other hazards. Annika's long blonde hair was pulled back in a severe bun hidden under a hat that draped down to cover the back of her neck. "And we're all carrying forty-pound rucksacks full of food, emergency medicine, clean socks and other necessities. If we actually find the hidden temple, I'm not sure how we will explore it. But at least we'll have clean underwear."

They continued walking in relative silence. Every hundred yards or so, Javier would pull an item out of his backpack and jam it into the ground. It looked like a foot-long piece of pencil-thin metal with a dark blue knob at the end. Javier stuck about half the length of the item into the dirt to his right without even missing a stride. This happened three or four times before it dawned on any of the academics what was going on. Dr. Crawford turned to Calvin and said:

"GPS markers. They're flagging our path. Probably for the escape route," he said with a dread smile.

Calvin nodded and looked around. Most of the team was simply trudging forward toward their goal. In what should be an exciting adventure, the joy was overcome by confusion and frustration mostly centered on their military escort.

**

The overwhelming heat and the dense jungle combined to make for a difficult trek. There were no hiking paths or Inca roads to follow. The four soldiers carried heavy-duty machetes to clear the path as best they could. The students walked in single-file and had quickly sweat through their clothes.

The team had walked just more than three miles of their ten-mile journey to the base of their target mountain. It had taken them close to two hours and it had rained three times during the trek. With the heat and humidity, all ten individuals were trying to stay hydrated. Even with all the sweat, it was time for a rest stop. Many would go off and urinate into bottles while many others would simply sit and rest for a moment. Half the academics needed to pee as well as one soldier. Three men went off the path they had followed to the right, while Annika, the lone female, moved off to the left.

"I want you to be comfortable, but you must stay close," Dario said as the team split in front of him. "There are dangers that even us tough guys cannot protect you from."

He had said this with a smile, but it quickly bled off his face as he turned to look at Edmundo, the guide bringing up the rear of the expedition. He simply nodded and held his left hand up toward the side of his head, thumb and pinkie extended to mimic a phone. The younger man returned the nod and slid off behind the trees.

"The goal would be fifty feet," Annika said, puffing, winding her way around some trees while filming. To her credit, she was watching where she was going rather than watching herself on the phone screen. "You'd want to get that far off the path before doing your business. However, we'll probably go about half that. Squat behind a tree and let 'er rip."

She reached behind her to unclasp a Gatorade bottle with a wide mouth from the underside of her backpack. Annika held it up to the camera.

"Not only is it uncouth to pee all over the place out in the open," she continued, wagging the bottle back and forth before dropping it out of the camera's view. "You know. The sanctity of the land. But also the smell of the urine, the salt content, could potentially attract dangerous animals. So the goal is to whoosh into the bottles and empty them in a stream or something."

Edmundo followed her at an angle so he would be out of the camera's line of sight. He was sure of Dario's goal in this situation, but unsure how to accomplish it. The video record of this excursion could not exist.

Annika found her spot, about twenty feet from the rest of the team. She turned off her recording and squatted against a tree. She uncapped the bottle and sighed. Twenty feet into the thick jungle might as well be twenty miles. For all intents and purposes, she was invisible and less worried about privacy than the utter annoyance of the experience.

Movement up and to the right caught Edmundo's attention. He kept coming, but slowed down and slid further to his left.

Annika bounced up and down a few times to capture any stray drops and sighed again as she capped the thick plastic bottle, stood and awkwardly pulled up her pants. She had stowed the bottle and grabbed her phone.

"With that unpleasantness . . ."

The movement above her head was sudden and vicious. Edmundo froze in his tracks, watching the scene unfold in front of him.

From the distinctive diamond pattern along its back, Edmundo quickly realized it was a bushmaster snake. The biggest pit viper in the world. Aggressive when it felt threatened, the snake must have somehow seen Annika as a challenge. Perhaps it had laid eggs nearby. Whatever the case, it had attacked from above and struck the exposed skin under Annika's chin, injecting directly into her throat and flooding the network of arteries and veins in her neck. The snake was ten feet long and began curling away to watch its prey for a reaction. Annika's hand went to her throat, dropping her phone as it continued to record, and she tried to scream. Only a crushed sound escaped her mouth, though, as the bushmaster's long fangs had punctured deep into her throat, injuring her vocal cords and immediately swelling the surrounding tissue.

Annika fell to the ground, eyes wide and legs kicking. The snake watched her and didn't see Edmundo leap forward and swipe downward at the reptile's head. He aimed about a foot behind its jaws and swung with all his might to ensure a death blow, lest the bushmaster turn its wrath upon the soldier. Edmundo decapitated the snake with his gleaming machete and the fear in Annika's face was replaced with a shred of hope. The soldier swiped the snake's head away with his weapon and crouched down in front of the girl.

They all had vials of antivenom in their emergency medical kits, but he simply paused. Annika, again, tried to scream for help. The man simply shook his head and put his left hand over her face completely covering her mouth and nose. She died terrified, kicking her legs and flailing her arms. As she went still, Edmundo cried out.

"I need help," he yelled over his shoulder, his gloved hand still on the student's face. "Quickly. It's the girl. I need help."

Dario and Dr. Crawford came crashing through the underbrush. They were the first to arrive, breathless, followed by the rest of the team.

"Oh my God," Crawford said. He kept looking back and forth from the headless ten-foot-long pit viper to the dead girl, so full of life only minutes ago. "Oh my God."

Her phone was nowhere to be found.

**

"I don't think you appreciate this situation," Dr. Crawford said. He had moved the group away from Annika's corpse. Her neck had swollen to huge proportions before she died and her eyes were completely red with broken blood vessels. Not only was it difficult to see a dead body – a close friend – the horror of her death was stitched across her face and throat.

Edmundo and Ramon were scouting the area looking for more danger that was hidden away. Javier and Dario stood with the five academics in a heated discussion.

"This young girl is dead, Dario," the professor continued. "We were responsible for her. This expedition is **over**." Javier stood stoic off Dario's right shoulder and slightly behind. Dario, for his part, stood his ground simply watching the professor, unsmiling.

Crawford was silent for a moment. The other two professors and the two students had made a loose semi-circle behind him. Doctors Hart and Del Campo were listening in on the conversation, but Jenny and Calvin were whispering quietly to each other. Sensing that it was his turn, Dario actually took a step forward to halve the distance between him and Crawford.

"No, Doctor," he said. "I don't think *you* appreciate the situation. You see, your student adventure has gained a significant amount of interest in many large, government offices. Whether you intended to or not, your request for access to our buried cultural treasures has, um, woke up a sense of national pride." He paused, the corners of his mouth quickly upturning and then flattening. Not a smile. Maybe a nervous flutter. "Possibly some greed if I can be honest to you."

The other two students had now turned and faced Dario from behind the three professors. The two military guides had also returned from their circuit of the area to stand behind the students. Two soldiers in front, two in the rear.

"If you truly uncover a hidden temple," he continued, "then we will pave a hiking path. An Inca Trail. Moche Path. Something. People will pay to visit. Plus gift shops. News reports across the world. It is a winning situation. We'll let you publish your papers … but the profit remains ours."

Now, a full grin as the realization dawned on Crawford.

"Money? Annika died for money?"

"No, no señor," Dario said. "She died because she was stupid. And didn't respect the jungle. How do you pause to urinate beneath a ten-foot snake with a diamond-pattern along its back?" There was a moment's pause.

"But we need to call her parents."

"No, no again, Dr. Crawford. She stays here. We go to our mountain. We grab her – what's left of her – on the way back. Our lap of victory, as you say. We will inform her parents of this horrible tragedy. Just not right now."

The entire team paused. No one said a word, running the scenario through their heads. Calvin finally turned around and saw the two soldiers, machetes still out, standing a few paces behind them. Finally, Dr. Crawford shook his head.

"This isn't right," he said. "I understand your point, but a young woman is dead. This excursion is officially on pause."

Dario only smiled.

"It's funny, amigo, that you think this is a debate."

Javier unholstered his pistol. Edmundo and Ramon stepped forward.

"This adventure continues," Dario said. "Take a moment. Grieve your loss. Shed your tears. We walk in sixty seconds."

**

They had hiked another three miles in absolute silence. The team fell back into the same format and rhythm as before Annika's tragic accident. Ramon and Javier in the lead followed by the five academics and trailed by Dario and Edmundo. The four soldiers had holstered their weapons, but all held machetes. While they certainly hacked at overgrown sections of the chosen path, it was clearly a posture chosen to remind the students that a challenge would not be tolerated.

"Okay," Dario said. "We break here. Have a protein bar. Urinate. Have a seat. We walk in ten minutes."

He had picked a nice spot. It was a small clearing, maybe the size of an average house – around 2,000 square feet. There were a few fallen trees and thick shrubs. Javier and Ramon immediately turned to their left to relieve themselves behind a tree while Dario and Edmundo stayed on watch. They would change positions when ready. Like the machetes, it was a clear message to the academics that they were under control. For their part, the five remaining academics walked to the opposite end of the clearing from Javier's group. They walked as a team of five.

"So, we just go back to back, right?" Calvin said, looking at his team. "Keep an eye out for each other."

"Uncomfortable, but necessary," Dr. Hart said, nodding.

They put a large shrub between themselves and Dario. He could still see them, although somewhat obstructed. Dr. Hart and Jenny Renard, shoulder to shoulder, crouched and relieved themselves into their personal containers. Calvin, Dr. Crawford and Dr. Del Campo remained standing, but they continued moving their eyes, always scanning their surroundings. Even if they had an inkling that Edmundo hadn't tried to help the dying Annika, the presence of the bushmaster snake was undeniable. They had to be on the lookout for everything from scorpions and giant centipedes to snakes and wild boars.

They finished and began walking back to the center of the clearing as a group. Professor Crawford walked with Calvin on one side and Remy Hart on the other. He spoke without moving his head to either side, but the words were directed at the group.

"Annika had been filming all day," he said in a low tone. "I didn't see her phone by her body. Did any of you?"

The rest of his team stayed silent but shook their heads.

"Do you think they killed her for it?" Dr. Hart asked.

"I don't know," Gus Del Campo said from behind her. "Maybe she recorded something she wasn't supposed to."

"Yeah," Calvin said. "Like our escorts themselves."

The implication of this filled the silence between the five walkers. Did the four soldiers plan on killing them and taking credit for the find? Were the academics always supposed to be a casualty of the jungle?

"Oh dear," Crawford said as the full implication of what could be going on started to dawn on him. "I'm so sorry for greenlighting this excursion."

Calvin shook his head.

"We'll be okay," he said, although he believed the absolute opposite to be true.

**

In the clearing, everyone milled about. The four soldiers stayed loosely together, laughing, eating snacks, but always watching their charges. The five academics had settled around the other end of one of the larger fallen trees. Professor Del Campo and Jenny Renard had sat down on it to rest their feet. Crawford and Hart stood off to the side talking. They were running back through the events of the day trying to guess if it was something on Annika's phone that had at worst led to her death and at best caused Edmundo to scoop it up as she lay expiring on the jungle floor.

For his part, Cal Woods simply leaned back, resting his butt against the huge trunk of the fallen tree. He was, in fact, snacking on a protein bar as Dario had suggested and rationing some water to stave off dehydration. They were more than halfway to what they had determined to be the final resting place of the mining village of San Pietro – sleeping in the shadow of Little Sister Peak.

After he finished his snack, he packed away the trash and stood up straight, stretching the muscles up and down his back. Leaning back against the fallen tree, Calvin closed his eyes and rubbed his face with his hands. He was momentarily disoriented when he reopened his eyes, however, as white spots danced in his vision. To clear the strange anomaly, he closed his eyes again – tightly. He shook his head from side to side and cracked his neck. Ready to test his vision, he opened his eyes again.

The four academics were staring at him.

"What?" he asked.

As if in slow motion, the student and three professors melted right in front of Cal. He didn't scream but jerked backward in shock. The four people had melted into what looked like a shadow, a puddle that was spreading outward from where their feet were. Panicked, he looked around. The four soldiers, who had just been across the small clearing, were now gone.

Cal took a halting step backward. Followed by another and another. He was looking at the puddle of people that seemed to continue spreading even when there were no more academics to melt. He nearly tripped as he backed up against a large boulder in the center of the clearing. The puddle of people stopped expanding and rested, pulsing, mere inches from Cal's feet. Suddenly, the puddle-shadow started retracting away from him. He could see, with this new movement, that it wasn't a puddle at all. Not a shadow. Not melted people.

Spiders.

A million spiders all collected in one small, condensed area. The spiders continued moving together and started piling up in the center of the huge dark spot. One pile. Then two. The two piles continued growing upward and then finally leaned together to form one big pile. An upside-down capital letter Y.

"No," Calvin said, the illusion suddenly becoming clear to his eyes.

The pile of spiders were building the shape of a human. Twenty feet away from him.

"No," he shouted at the pile of arachnids, louder this time.

The group of spiders had two legs, a torso, two arms and now a head. While there was no detail, and no definition, the spider pile mimicked the posture of Calvin. He raised his right hand and rubbed his eyes as if they were still playing tricks on him. Slower, and with no detail, the Spider Calvin made the same movement.

"No," he screamed.

As if in bemused response, the Spider Calvin yelled back – with no sound. His back pressed up against the boulder, Cal watched as his shadow-self began to expand and grow and morph. Additional arms and legs sprouted from the body. The torso fattened and elongated.

"Oh no," Cal said.

The dark Calvin suddenly leaned forward and stood on its eight legs. A true spider. Thirteen feet tall and more than thirty feet long. Cal Woods screamed and started running through the clearing. He didn't look back as he made it back to the makeshift trail the team had been following in the direction of San Pietro.

His legs became heavy, his lungs started burning. Breathing hurt, but he couldn't stop to rest. He didn't turn his head, but Calvin could hear the giant spider crashing through the jungle behind him. Small trees fell. Underbrush was flattened. Somehow buried in the middle of all these sounds, Calvin could hear a click clack click sound as if old, dried sticks were being knocked together, the sound a box of drumsticks would make if they were upended across the floor … but, somehow, organized. A rhythm.

"You're nearly there," came a voice deep inside Calvin's head. He rounded a corner, into another small clearing. There was a river to his right and what was left of a roughly-hewn road to his left. Straight ahead – Little Sister.

"Home," came the voice.

"No," Calvin screamed, but no sound came out.

** **

He was being shook by Professor Crawford. As his vision cleared, Calvin could make out his advisor, but he couldn't hear anything. He could see Crawford's mouth moving, but there was no sound. Slowly, as his vision cleared his other senses started to wake up.

He was sitting on the ground, in the clearing with the boulder and fallen tree. The other academics were crowded around Dr. Crawford. The four soldiers were slowly advancing on the group, unsure what to make of the situation.

" - you okay?" Dr. Crawford had his hands on Cal's shoulders, gently shaking him awake.

"Yeah, yeah," Cal said. "Please stop that." He blinked hard. "What happened?"

"I don't know," Crawford said, standing up and holding his hand down to Cal to help him stand as well. "You were rubbing your face, then started stumbling backward. Shouted the word NO two or three times. And fell on your keister."

Jenny had joined Dr. Crawford and likewise held her hand down to help Calvin up.

"Thank you," Cal said as he reached up, his right hand offered to his advisor and his left toward his fellow student. "I must have fallen asleep. Nightmare."

Fully standing, Calvin shook his head, stretched his arms above his head and cracked his spine back and forth.

"Wow," he said.

"Thank you for the entertainment, amigo," Dario said, as the four escorts had joined the students.

"With the excitement over, we should take up the trail, no?"

**

The team settled back into their same pattern and speed. Edmundo replaced Ramon at the head of the group to continue hacking at small branches in their path. Other than that change to combat arm fatigue, everyone was in line. There were a few sideways glances thrown, of course, toward Calvin.

The nine adventurers had trekked an additional mile into the jungle on a north-easterly path toward the map location of Little Sister, and the section of the slope where Cal had expected the ruins of San Pietro.

Edmundo slowed his pace and the rest of the team followed suit.

"¡Más despacio!" he said quietly over his right shoulder. In response, Javier held up his right hand, fingers splayed, as a signal to those toward the back of the group. "Slow down."

Jenny looked back at Calvin, who shrugged his shoulders. She had a furrowed brow and squinted her eyes as their pace forward became almost a crawl.

"It sounds like chewing," she finally said.

**

As they trudged forward, it started raining yet again, and the chewing stopped. Ramon joined

Edmundo at the front and the two men scouted ahead to locate the source.

Suddenly, there was a horrible screeching sound as a wild boar darted out of the trees and underbrush to their right and ran across the team's path. The feral animal was more than four feet long from snout to tail and easily weighed two hundred pounds. Once across the path, the boar paused and turned back toward the team. It seemed to assess the humans as threats. Without pausing, Javier ran forward with his machete. Startled by the huge man, the boar turned again and ran into some heavy underbrush. Undeterred, Javier followed.

The team heard squeals, crashes and grunts. After two long minutes, a slightly disheveled Javier slowly emerged from the trees. The machete dripped blood. He walked back into the path and stood directly in front of Calvin, taking his place in line without saying a word. The soldier was clearly a head taller than the student. Javier was breathing hard and Cal willed himself not to look at the gore dripping from the two-foot-long blade.

After a tense moment, Javier simply turned his head and spat upon the ground.

"Okay, okay," Dario said walking to the head of the group. "Time to get moving. You get famous. We get rich."

With that, he whistled and waved his right hand in a circular motion above his head.

"Vamos."

FIVE

They never saw the remains of the wild boar and they did not expect to see Annika again – give her a proper burial. The five academics continued walking forward, in a straight line, following their guide and the giant soldier, Javier.

Imagination is a terrible and powerful tool. Without speaking to each other, the five adventurers were creating horrifying scenarios in their heads. None of them, now, expected to survive the trip. It was becoming obvious in their minds that the plan all along was for them to be casualties of the jungle. Javier continued to place GPS markers at regular intervals. There was no doubt that the soldiers would bury the bodies – all of them – in shallow graves where they might be either eaten or quickly decomposed by the jungle. The ground was so full of life it almost seemed to pulsate. The three professors and two students were silent in their depression, but continued to march forward – hoping for a different outcome, but not expecting it.

Two more hours of walking and they crested a small hill into a huge clearing. And there she was.

The Little Sister.

"Oh my God," Dr. Hart said, looking up at the face of the mountain. "It's beautiful."

It was the final peak of a long mountain range that ran through Eastern Peru from the north to the south. Due to its position in the jungle and surrounding foothills, the peak was somehow obstructed from view. It was almost as if the Little Sister was hiding.

The group all paused and took in the sight. Even the four soldiers seemed to be overcome with shock. The scene, ringed by huge trees, backdropped by blue skies, punctuated by puffy white clouds, was overwhelming.

"Madre," Dario said under his breath.

And then, after a moment, he turned to Crawford.

"Okay," the soldier said. "Let's find your village."

**

It was eerie, the feeling of solitude that swept over the team of nine. They stood roughly one hundred yards south of what was left of a clearing. They could see some ruins. The broken footprint of San Pietro. To the right, the crumbling remains of a larger building. Behind it and to the left the backdrop of the final peak of the mountain range. Pac-Falness. Little Sister. Chosen as hallowed ground hundreds – perhaps thousands – of years ago.

To their right was the remains of a road that curved along with the river that lay just a little further right. The river and road both curved away into the distance, both north and south. Both must have disappeared further south into the jungle as the hiking party didn't pass either of them on the way to the city.

The river, potentially, could eventually meet with the Amazon hundreds of miles north. The road north? There was no way to tell.

"How is any of this still here?" Dario asked absently. Most shocking was that some buildings stood nearly complete while others were mostly destroyed.

Dr. Hart shrugged.

"They've done studies on the reclamation of abandoned cities and structures," she said. "It depends on a number of factors. The materials used. The stability of the ecosystem. Is the area prone to earthquakes? Structures will topple relatively quickly. Were the structures built using steel and glass? They might only last five or six decades. Stone structures could last hundreds of years."

Dario nodded, his eyes sweeping the ruins of San Pietro.

"I like it," he said, smiling. "It sounds like you are starting to write your article, no?"

It was late in the afternoon, and it was time to eat a proper meal for the first time since breakfast. Everyone, however, was too excited about reaching their destination and started moving forward as a group.

"Hold on," Crawford said. "We should start documenting in earnest. But we should also eat something. We take a short break here and start in thirty minutes?" He asked this last bit looking directly at Dario, who nodded in response.

"Yes, of course," the soldier responded and then barked a short order at his three troopers.

**

The academics had all packed selections of Meal Ready-to-Eat (MRE) packages for food. Some required heated water, some could be eaten dry, some needed simple water mix-ins. Each of the five had selected a package and bottle of water. They sat in a group eating; some quiet conversation took place. The four soldiers, likewise, had packed MREs, but they looked truly military-grade.

"San Pietro," Professor Crawford said and smiled. He had finished his meal and bent the empty package into a small square before sealing it in a Ziplock bag full of his trash from the hike. There were a couple empty bottles of water and some protein bar wrappers in there.

"Dr. Crawford?" Calvin asked.

The professor looked at his student.

"I'm not sure why the connection never appeared to me before now," he said. The other academics were, likewise, folding up and discarding their late lunches. "You remember studying the Crusades?" Calvin nodded, but there wasn't a significant response from the others. "In the 11th century, numerous bloody, horrific battles were fought between the Christians and Muslims. Holy wars fought to secure control of sacred sites that were crucial to both groups. Generally, there are eight crusades – separate holy wars fought – although some split the eighth into two parts, making for a ninth war. I prefer to keep the official number at eight. But that's neither here nor there."

He took a sip from his water and cleared his throat. Edmundo had turned to look at the group of academics.

"I digress. Partly due to popular media, and partly due to a conflation of events, many people only really have heard of the Children's Crusade. Without knowing what it was. People think that the church enlisted children, as those pure of heart, to engage the Muslims on the battlefield. Many use this as a horrific example of backward thinking. Arguments against the church. In truth, what is traditionally seen as the Children's Crusade is actually two separate events that happened at nearly the same time.

"A shepherd in Germany, Nicolas, gathered a group of more than 20,000 believers and led them across the Alps into Italy. He claimed to have had a vision from God that the sea would dry up and allow them to march into the Holy Land. They would preach the Good Word to the Muslims who would immediately be converted to Catholicism. While many people gave up and went home, more than 60 percent of the believers perished on the trip. Around 7,000 people arrived at the port city of Genoa only to find that the sea had not, in fact, dried up. The Genoese authorities offered the crusaders citizenship, partly out of pity and partly out of astonishment of their convictions. Many took it. Nicolas did not. He died on his way back home, attempting to cross the Swiss Alps a second time.

"The second account actually had something to do with children," he continued. Three of the soldiers had stopped chatting and were listening to the story. Only Javier continued eating, not paying attention to the history lesson.

"Stephen of Cloyes, a 12-year-old French boy, claimed that he had a letter for the king of France from Jesus Himself. He attracted large groups of youths, adults and children – more than 30,000 individuals of all ages. They marched first to Saint Denis and then all across France, spreading their message. However, more than half his initial followers became disillusioned and returned home. Eventually, Stephen's group of followers, greatly diminished and largely comprised of juvenile Crusaders, made it to Marseilles where they continued to preach and survived by begging for food. It was here that the group almost totally disbanded with the juveniles, begging their way home to their families.

"Nothing too exciting, right?" the professor asked, smiling. "These stories are combined in an interesting way. A young boy from Germany has a vision directly from Jesus. *You can peacefully convert the Muslims*, Jesus promises. *I will part the sea and you can march to the Holy Land.* The young boy marches his 30,000 followers to the Mediterranean Sea, which does not part. The children are sold to two merchants who promise them free passage to start a new life. Unfortunately, it all ends in tears. Half the children are taken to Tunisia and sold into slavery. The other half die in a shipwreck during an unexpected windstorm.

"They died against the rocks ringing San Pietro Island on the west coast of Sardinia. Isola di San Pietro," he stopped and smiled to himself. "This tale and the tale of Little Sister Mountain are wholly unrelated, but the name always, somehow, sounded familiar to me."

**

It painted a strange picture. The ruins of the village in the foreground. What appeared to be the mining complex behind that. Looming over everything as a giant, shaded background was the peak of Little Sister. The team had finished their break period and started to move into the mining town of San Pietro.

There was a path that led through the town and wound around the eastern slope of the peak. It was smaller and more overgrown than the road that ran along the outside of the town, separating San Pietro from the river. The grouped buildings were in various states of disrepair but hadn't all totally collapsed due to the strength of stone and brick construction. They ran in three columns with the two on the far left looking like residential buildings – on one side of the small path – and the other side of the path were fewer, but larger buildings. Likely commercial properties. Retail, even, or small industry. As the city grew, obviously, there would be a greater need for all three types of property – residential, commercial, industrial. Unfortunately, San Pietro never really grew past its initial population spurt.

The division of labor was such that the two students were taking notes and making sketches while the three professors were snapping pictures and recording video of everything around them.

"It is the mountain, no?" Dario asked, walking alongside Dr. Crawford. "That brought you to my small corner of the world? I read your report, but was ordered here by my superiors. They assured me that it was the mountain that was of importance."

Professor Crawford nodded.

"The village of San Pietro is an oddity," he said, "as there was a city of people who suddenly vanished. Or, more correctly, were murdered. There was an account from a group of Christian Missionaries on a scheduled stop, a journal entry by a brother, who noted that the village was horrific beyond belief. And the team of religious officials left without further inquiry."

"The entire town murdered," Dario repeated somewhat quietly.

"Yes," the professor responded. "A map puts the town right here, in the shadow of the mountain. Calvin found an older account of the mountain. A mythology. A claim that there is a natural cavern inside the peak. Huge. And the Mochican high priests built a temple there."

"Inside the mountain," Dario said, as if trying to wrap his head around the concept.

"Yes, apparently," continued the professor. "Possibly to their warrior deity. The Decapitator. The Spider God."

"Terrific," Ramon said quietly. He had been walking behind the two men listening but looking around the buildings – scanning for danger hidden around any corner.

"Quite," said the professor, looking at one building, mostly standing, with three long grooves cut down it from the roof to the ground. They looked like claw marks, but not exactly. "Quite."

**

The majority of the structures were either destroyed or had been reclaimed by nature over the last hundred years. That said, the team of nine walked up and down the small streets examining everything. They were taking notes, recording video, recording audio and snapping dozens of pictures each. The academics seemed more excited about the adventure while the four-man security team all seemed to be checking their watches and looking at the looming specter of Little Sister Mountain as it was their final destination.

"This was a saloon," Calvin said, quietly, to himself.

"What was that?" Professor Hart had been standing near him and heard the short phrase even though it wasn't meant for anyone else to hear.

"Oh, sorry," Calvin said as he snapped one more photo on his camera. "I said that this was probably a saloon."

Hart looked right and left, up and down the street. She then backed up a few steps and took a good look at the ruin in front of her. Finally, she shrugged and looked back at him.

"Why would you say that?" She took the few steps back to the front of the building to stand next to Calvin. "I'm not sure I see any outward signs of what this building was."

Calvin looked at her. He had taken one of Dr. Hart's archaeology courses during his long tenure at the university. She always struck him as bright, observant and well-read. He blushed.

"I don't know," he said. "I'm sorry. Just a guess, really."

In truth, Calvin had remembered a portion of his brief hallucination in the jungle – seeing people fleeing from the building when it was lit up for evening customers, a sign out front with alcohol iconography on it. But he couldn't tell her this or she'd think he was crazy.

"A guess," Hart repeated and nodded. "Okay."

"Hey, look at this," Jenny called from two buildings down the street, and to the left.

Calvin and Hart looked at each other and then struck off to find the other student.

**

The five academics and Dario had all congregated inside one of the small buildings they felt were likely miners' residences. It was in an average state of disrepair – the majority of the walls were intact, but the roof was completely gone. As such, the interior of the structure was carpeted with leaves, branches and other debris that would have blown in with the wind and storms that punctuated the weather for the last nine decades.

Jenny and Crawford had been the first into this building and it was Jenny who had called out to collect the team. These two individuals were kneeling in a corner of the building, ringed by the rest of the team.

"I almost didn't see it," Jenny said. She was crouched before a small stone box wedged into the corner of the room. It was clear that the item was originally covered with leaves and twigs before she brushed the debris off. The box was only two feet by two feet with a two-inch stone lid covering it.

"Here, let me help," Calvin said as he stepped in and crouched down in front of the box. Jenny grabbed one side of the lid and Cal grabbed the other as they slid the hunk forward and off the top of the box. They rested it carefully on the dirt floor of the home and peered inside. Crawford clicked on a powerful flashlight and shone it into the small area.

"Wow," Jenny said.

The small stone box was nearly half-filled with small items. They were stone carvings and metal statuettes. There were some wood carvings and some of the items even had inlaid jewels. The small totems ranged in material and artistry, but it was clear they were collected, coveted and protected by the owner.

"Now, that's strange," Hart said, leaning forward. Everyone in the room paused for a moment to give her a chance to collect her thoughts and explain her reaction. She crouched in between Jenny and Cal; Crawford shifted so the beam of light still illuminated the contents of the stone box.

Hart picked up a small, sturdy branch from the floor of the hut and pointed to one structure in the box.

"From what I read during our prep, this figure is common to the Moche religion," It was a circular trinket about three inches across. It was a carving of a face in profile. Half the trinket was light with clean lines and half was darkened by small, cross-hatched carvings. It was vaguely reminiscent of the Chinese yin-yang symbol representing the duality of nature.

"Si, the moon goddess," Crawford said. "Common, both to Moche and Incan."

"Exactly," Hart continued, moving her stick to point at another item. "And this is a statue of the Egyptian God Anubis. There is almost no reason these two items should be in close proximity. Possibly there were collectors of religious artifacts in the 1800s, but in a small mining village in Peru? Seems a little strange."

"This is also Egyptian," Crawford had bent forward and highlighted another statuette with the beam of his flashlight. He slid the beam to the left. "This, a Chinese serpent. It looks dusty, but it could be carved out of jade. And this. It looks like a capital T. Quite similar to the monoliths found at the Gobekli Tepe excavation. You have a chapter on them, right Cal?"

Calvin nodded.

"Yessir. It's almost identical. Right down to the slope of the cross." He thought for a moment. "There's no mistaking it."

Hart gently moved around some pieces with her pointer, reluctant to actually touch anything.

"A bizarre collection," she said and stood up. "I could spend the rest of the day here, but I understand we have a larger purpose. It might be a mystery to us, but it could also simply amount to a coin or stamp collection. If we found a box of coins from different parts of the world and different eras in my grandfather's closet, it might be a strange find for us, but it's completely explainable. Unfortunately, the person who collected these items died in 1853."

"Let's take some close-up photos and swing back through when we have time to extract, bag and label everything," Crawford said, shutting off his light and leaning back from the group.

Cal nodded in response.

"I like your analogy of the coin collection, Dr. Hart," Cal said, also standing and stepping back. "But it also brings up the idea of different eras. People think they happened pretty close together – with the benefit of historical hindsight or a blurb in a textbook. But the truth is that many of these epochs lasted a significant amount of time. I remember reading an article that sort of mentioned casually, in passing, that what we think of in general as "Ancient Egypt" lasted several thousand years. The fact that in Ancient Egypt there were actually archaeologists studying monuments that were already thousands of years old."

Jenny had also stood and stepped back from the stone box.

"Yep," Hart said. "Ramses II was the third Pharoah of the 19th dynasty. He ruled from 1279 to 1213 BC. Known for building the gigantic temples at Abu Simbel, he was also known for researching, studying and repairing monuments that were already a thousand years old. The Sphinx is commonly dated from around 2500 BC. The Bent Pyramid at Dashur was erected around the same time. Both 1300 years before Ramses II was even born."

They made mental notes to return to this area after getting a look at the mountain. The team found nothing else of note while exploring San Pietro.

**

It was late in the afternoon, and they decided to get into the mountain before it got too dark. If the area seemed safe, they could even camp out in the old mine tunnels to avoid the elements.

"Do they have bears in Peru?" Jenny asked, mentally running through cave-borne dangers as they left the final mining camp building.

"Sure," Dr. Del Campo said. "The spectacled bear is about six feet tall and maybe 250 pounds.

They are pretty much vegetarians, but will probably fight if they need to."

"Great," Jenny said.

The team had crossed the remains of the main road that disappeared off to the north and now stood on the main path from San Pietro to Little Sister. Calvin paused to look to his right, down to the shell of the mining town, and then to his right to watch the footpath wind up against the lower sections of the mountain. Even from this low vantage point, he could see that the path led directly to the opening of a cave.

"Yeah, great," he said to himself. Javier put his huge hand on Cal's right shoulder and nudged him forward. Despite the assurances the team had received from Dario, the shock of Annika's death was still fresh in his mind – and the way the military men forced the excursion to continue for the betterment of the region. Was this really all about fame and money for the area?

As a group, the team continued to walk up the path, Javier continued as before to place the small GPS locators to the right of the line they followed. During their voyage, he had used just more than three-quarters of his supply – which had just about turned out to be the right measurement.

The path took an ever-increasing upward angle and the team quickly started huffing for breath, their gait dramatically impacted. The mouth of the cave yawned open before them, a broken-tooth scream that seemed to be framed by foliage and some collapsed trees. Greenery, however, had started to wither away from the general area. Calvin had the strange notion that this was the jungle's version of landscaping around an important building's façade or a famous person's home in an affluent neighborhood.

He smiled to himself, running through countless episodes of real estate and renovation shows he had watched. "Curb appeal," he said to himself as they reached the cave entrance.

"It's strange," Professor Crawford said. "Like a hybrid between man-made and a natural formation. I bet this cave existed and the miners carved and refined it to their needs."

The five academics stood at the precipice with the four soldiers behind them.

"I don't understand," Calvin said.

"It's called an adit," Professor Del Campo said. "It's a horizontal path that miners carve for a number of reasons. Ventilation. Drainage. An auxiliary entrance. Usually it runs horizontal across subsurface shafts." He peered into the adit with a strong flashlight. "Strange. I don't see anything, though. It just looks like a corridor in an office building. No doors or windows, though. Just a straight, relatively featureless hallway."

All nine team members affixed strong battery-powered headlamp flashlights to their foreheads and also activated high-powered flashlights. They carefully stepped into the mining adit and began slowly walking along the path.

"Is there any reason to believe this leads to your temple?" Dario asked.

Calvin shook his head.

"Not really," he said. "But it seems related, at least. If this doesn't pan out, we'll have to start searching for another natural entrance into the mountain."

They could see that the passage was a few hundred feet long before it terminated at the far end. There were equally-spaced supports that still seemed to be in fairly good shape even after all the time that had elapsed. None of the team members voiced any safety concerns, but there was a foreboding sense of the unknown. The natural reaction to a completely foreign environment. Utter darkness. And a slight sense of claustrophobia.

After just more than one hundred yards, they reached the end of the tunnel. They had seen no branching paths, no vertical shafts.

"Shit," Edmundo said under his breath.

They had traveled 300 feet toward the center of a mountain and the passage simply ended.

"Quite," Dr. Crawford agreed. "I suppose we can go back out and continue around the eastern face of Little Sister. Make a circuit around it."

"Hang on," Calvin said.

He had started back down the adit toward the entrance. This time, he was walking slowly, near the inside wall of the tunnel. He held his flashlight in his right hand at a dramatic angle while running his left hand along the stone wall. He stopped and then reversed direction for six or seven feet and then stopped again. Cal seemed to be examining a portion of the wall when the rest of the team caught up to him. They all shined their flashlights and headlamps at the section.

"This looks like a doorway that's been filled in," Calvin said. He ran his hand up what looked like it could be the seam of the two sections on the left. It extended just above his head, at around seven feet, and then moved to the right, before finally coming back down vertically to the floor. It made a haphazard shape – like an accidental doorway that branched off the adit.

They lacked any heavy mining tools, but there were some big rocks strewn about the area. Javier picked one up that must have weighed close to fifty pounds. Dario shrugged as the big man looked at him.

"Try it," he said.

Javier whirled like an Olympic shot-putter and heaved the stone right into the center of the makeshift doorway. The patchwork largely held, but it cracked, and it sounded like a hollow thud when it impacted. Encouraged, Javier picked up the large stone again, and hit the wall with it. This time a small hole appeared. The big soldier did this three more times before pausing to catch his breath. He was sweating now, and rested his hands on his knees. The other three soldiers went to work pushing stones out of the broken wall into the passage beyond. When the hole reached almost three-feet-square, work stopped as Dario peeked in.

"It looks like another passage," Dario said. "Like this one." He peered in, sweeping his light from the left to the right and back. Finally, he pulled his head back out. "Feels a little warm. And smells bad. Broken." He stepped back and nodded to Javier, who had finally gotten his breath back.

The big man stepped up to the wall flanked by Ramon and Edmundo. The three of them started pushing in on the sides of the constructed wall, careful to avoid the top of the structure caving in on them. After a few minutes of effort, the wall toppled inward and fell into the off-shoot passage.

"Wow," Dr. Hart said.

**

It was a study in opposites. The passageway was wider than the adit, but also shorter. It looked man-made as the sides were smooth to the touch. Almost as if they had been carved and then polished to a high sheen. The floor, however, looked natural and unadorned. It was uneven dirt and rock in direct contrast to the walls. There were supports placed every few yards, but they had been painstakingly blended into the wall so instead of appearing to be separate units, they looked like small bumps in the smooth surface.

Most striking, however, were the intricate carvings that made up the entire left-hand side of the passage.

"Amazing," Professor Crawford said, leaning in to take a closer look at the carvings. "I can't tell if it's ornate or a pictogram. Gus, does this look like any language you've seen?"

Del Campo leaned forward, adjusting the angle of his headlamp. After a few moments, he shook his head, still bent in close to the wall.

"No," he said, finally. "It looks strictly ornate. Almost a landscape scene. I'm sure it's ultimately telling a story, but we'd have to take numerous photos and maybe digitally stitch them together."

Crawford nodded in response and leaned back, standing up straight and turning back to face the other academics.

"I'm going to take a bunch of pictures of this wall," he said. "Calvin, why don't you follow along with me so we have two sets? Then we can keep going. I don't want to skip over any type of discovery for fear that we might lose track and forget to come back to it."

There was a silent moment as the team seemed to consider this as a whole. Finally, Dario nodded.

"You are right, Dr. Crawford," he said. "We should document as we go. Only I'd like Ramon to take the second set of pictures."

He nodded to Ramon who took a camera out of his backpack and walked to the head of the hallway with Crawford. They started taking pictures, one after the other. First the top, then the bottom, then move six feet to the right and repeat. The entire process took only five minutes, and it took them to the far end of the passage.

The end of the passage was closed off. It was sealed, similar to the small wall they had just crashed through from the adit, but not the same. Dario got close to the wall and peered at it with his strong headlamp. He ran his right hand along the surface and then crouched to the floor of the tunnel.

"It feels like mud," he announced to the collected group. "More like the floor, here, than the walls. Quickly built."

Like he did with the wall, Dario ran his hand along the tunnel floor.

"There are deep grooves carved into the floor, here."

Edmundo and Calvin both crouched to look as well. Everyone shone their lights at the ground. There were dozens of what looked like scrape marks, several feet long, all leading from several yards away seemingly into the mud wall. The three men stood and all took a step back. Dario nodded to Ramon who took several steps back into the passage. After a deep exhale, he ran forward and dropped his shoulder into the mud wall like a rugby player. Ramon had expected to simply bounce off, so he guarded himself against serious injury ... however, his momentum carried him forward and the mud wall shattered around him. He fell forward into a giant cavern that expanded in all directions from the floor they now stood on.

"Oh my God," Professor Remy Hart said.

SIX

The team was shocked by the size and scope of the chamber. A city block full of skyscrapers could have easily fit inside the blank zone. It was as if the entire top half of the mountain had been scooped out and a lid placed back on top. There were a dozen or so shafts of light that seemed to shine down from the cracked peak of Little Sister Mountain. They were well-placed, illuminating the enormous space just enough to give a sense of size. The ceiling of the cavern looked like it was draped with cloth much like the top of a canopy bed. However, when the gentle breeze from the adit caught this material, it became clear that they were spider webs that covered the entire cavern.

Perhaps even more shocking than the gigantic cavern and the webbed ceiling was what occupied the center of the area – a ziggurat.

"Santa mierda," Edmundo said.

All nine people were shining their powerful flashlights around the cavern while their headlamps were also sending beams of white light into the gloom. They all stood in a tight cluster only a few yards into the hollow mountain from the mouth of the passage.

"Yeah," Dr. Hart said. She stepped forward away from the team toward the building.

While it was almost impossible to gauge the size of the stone temple in the vast emptiness of the cavern, as the team stepped closer and closer, it continued to rise before them.

"Looks to be about fifty or sixty feet high," Calvin said.

Dr. Hart nodded.

"It's a ziggurat," she said. "Like a blunted, step pyramid. That little building at the very top? That's the actual temple. The true holy area."

Everyone followed her gaze upward. There were three main levels not including the stone building on top. Each level was smaller in footprint, but taller in height than the one preceding it. In front of them was a huge double-door and the face of the building was lined with unlit torches. Leading away from the central entrance were two sets of stairs, one going to the left and one going to the right. It looked like these might be the only way to reach the upper floors as the stairs slowly ascended across the front of the building and around each side. Based on the angle of elevation and the sheer size of the structure, the steps likely met at the rear of the ziggurat – in the middle of the space – directly behind the temple atop the building.

"It's beautiful," Calvin said.

"Something's wrong here," Professor Hart muttered.

**

The five academics stood in front of the huge double-doors at the center base of the structure. The four soldiers took a short walk to the edges of the building. There were six torches lined along the front and they took the time to light each one. They seemed ceremonial rather than functional, but still provided pools of light around the immediate area. The lights illuminated a long, unbroken landscape carving along the front of the ziggurat. It didn't seem as detailed as the carved panels in the tunnel leading into the void, but the images were impossible to ignore.

"What do you mean?" Dr. Crawford said.

"It's a bit of a mashup, isn't it?" she said. "What everyone thinks of as a ziggurat is largely based on imagery from ancient Mesopotamia. They were enormous structures built to honor the city's chief deity. That smaller structure on top?" She pointed to the top center of the building. "That's the actual temple. The shrine. There's probably a statue or many statues placed in reverence to the deity."

She was silent, her eyes roaming the structure.

"The Incan temples that dot South America were built in a similar, but decidedly different, style. While they were step pyramids – meaning each level was smaller than the one below it rather than smooth like the pyramids at Giza – their dominant feature was a huge central staircase. It would have led directly from the middle base to the very top. These stairs, however, are quite ornate and sweep up and back from the face of the building. It is a strange architectural message."

"Okay," Crawford said, looking at the temple the entire time she was speaking.

"But, the door," she continued. "A ziggurat is a solid structure. The temple at the top would have an interior, of course, but the rest of the building should have a solid mud core. With baked bricks around the outer edges to provide a certain level of stability, but, really, it's all decorative. Some step pyramids might have chambers that the priests would use for storage, maintenance or even resting. But this doesn't look like that. It's possible there are matching entrances around the other three sides, but this huge central door looks rather imposing."

"The whole building is like a statue," Calvin said, nodding. "Solidly built. Created to inspire awe. It's not like a house. Or a church."

"Exactly," Dr. Hart said. "So, these doors would be worthless in the traditional structure. But here we are." She knelt in the dirt and ran her fingers along curved scrapes in the floor of the cavern. "These doors open, at least. They are functional rather than decorative. I don't know what's behind them, but they open outward. And have in the past."

"So, it stands to reason," Dr. Del Campo said, leaning in and touching the doors, "that, at least theoretically, there's something *inside* this building?"

Professor Hart stood up and ran her fingertips along the crack that divided the two doors. She only answered by nodding.

"Wild," Calvin said. "We should go in."

Remy Hart took a step back and looked up over the lip of the first level of the giant structure.

"I wonder if we shouldn't start at the top and work our way back down?"

The four soldiers had joined the academics at the doors.

"It's quite large," Dario said, looking up from the base to the temple. "These are the only stairs. They circle the structure and meet again at the back."

Dr. Crawford nodded. He stepped to his right and mounted the first few stairs, then stopped. Something had caught his attention. A shadow. Darker darkness stacked within the darkness.

"Are those...?" he started and then stopped.

Dario peered to his right to see what the professor had seen. He nodded in response, smiling.

"Yes, they are," he said. "Around the cavern there are four spokes. Or caves. Entrances to something at least. Not including the one we entered through."

"Whoa," Jenny Renard gasped. "Could there be four more of these … things?"

Dario shrugged.

"We did not explore," he said. "Just saw them."
He paused for a moment, looking, again, at the
building's façade and then the temple resting atop
the ziggurat. "Let's go," he said, grinning.

**

The team went up the stairs in the same order
they had hiked through the jungle. Two soldiers,
academics, two soldiers. As they could tell from
looking at the outside of the structure, the stairs
went along the front of the building, traversed the
entire side, and then half the back of the ziggurat. It
was a kind yet relentless incline, and everyone was
breathless by the time they reached the summit.

They were at the back of the ziggurat, on the
precipice of the topmost layer.

"Hmm," Jenny said.

Calvin looked over at her.

"What's that?" he asked.

"I have an odd habit of counting when I'm going
up or down stairs. Mostly up. I think it has
something to do with fatigue. Or boredom. I don't
know," she paused for breath, suddenly blushing a
bit – ashamed of her strange personality trait.
"There are ninety-one steps from the very first one.
We snaked across the front, the side and the back.
Ninety-one steps."

"Okay," Hart said.

"Assuming it's the same on the other side," she
continued, "that's one-hundred-and-eighty-two.

And look at that." She pointed at the small stair that led from the main rooftop surface into the ziggurat shrine.

No one spoke for a moment. They weren't understanding her inspiration.

"It's a half-step. One-hundred-and-eighty-two-point-five," again, Jenny paused to see if the others caught up. "It's exactly half a year. Three-hundred-and-sixty-five days divided by two is one-hundred-and-eighty-two-point-five . Ninety-one to a side and the half-step." Finally, she shrugged. "Not sure what the significance would be. There's really no way to track the sun inside a hollow mountain, but I just thought it was interesting."

The other four academics nodded, quietly thinking what the significance of the number could be. Finally, it was Dario who broke them out of their trance.

"Whoa," he said.

Everyone turned to follow his gaze. There was a small channel built into the bricks that lined the rooftop. He had crouched to look at it and saw that it was full of a dark-colored gelatinous substance. Still in the crouch, he looked up at Edmundo, who only shrugged in response. Dario had a lopsided grin and pulled a match out of his pocket. It was a part of the same waterproof package he had used to light the torches at the base of the temple.

"Do you think you should do that?" Crawford asked, concerned. "This building was likely erected

1500 years ago. Perhaps longer. Who knows what might happen?"

"Sin agallas, no hay gloria," he said, smiling. "Isn't that what you say? No guts, no glory? Nothing ventured, nothing gained? Live a little, my friend."

With a wide grin, Dario lit the match and touched it to the goop in the small crevasse. The result was impressive.

Fire.

The goo ignited and snaked all around the top level of the ziggurat. Once it reached the full circle, it lit the same channel that was inlaid around the edge of the stairs. From their perspective walking, they could not have seen the small cracks. The walls of the structure were cast in an eerie glow.

"Wow," Calvin said. "It must be crude oil or some mixture. How could it remain viable for so long?"

"We should note it and maybe get a sample," Crawford said. "Amazing."

The team stood rooted to the spot for a few moments. Finally, Dario, who had initially lit the mysterious chemical, shrugged off his backpack and opened it. He rummaged a bit toward the bottom on the pack and pulled out a small cylindrical item. He put the backpack down near his feet and started unfolding the contraption. The sections snapped into place and Cal could see that it was a small campsite shovel.

Dario saw him looking and smiled and grinned at the same time. He walked over to the flaming channel and quickly slid the shovel along the fire, scooping a small amount of the goop out and splashing it against the corner of the structure. The fire popped and sizzled but never went out. The goopy mixture slowly slid down the wall, still flaming, but acted on by gravity. It left a small fire trail until it puddled on the floor. It seemed to have the consistency of a very thick milkshake. Or well-blended peanut butter.

"Interesting," Crawford said, watching it all.

Dario wiped the spade end of the shovel off in the dirt that had accumulated near the base of the temple and turned back to the others, shrugging.

Everyone, at the same time, turned to look toward the shrine. It seemed that the burning oil was either timed or specifically designed to light the topmost structure last. Like a great beast emerging from the darkness, its features illuminated by pure flame, a giant spider crouched at the far end of the huge temple.

"Astonishing," Del Campo said. He stepped closer to the statue. "That statue. It looks black. Is it volcanic rock? Obsidian? Onyx? It's beautiful."

The team slowly advanced toward the shrine – itself the size of a small house. It was nearly fifty-feet-square with a twenty-foot ceiling. There were intricate carvings all around the columns that made up much of the walls of the enormous room. It looked to be one chamber, dominated by the crouching Spider God. After a few silent moments, they all stood just outside the main entrance that faced the rear of the cavern – the point where the two staircases converged. All nine had stopped – the five academics in front and the four soldiers behind and slightly flanking them.

"Is that," Cal said, "you don't suppose that's supposed to be life-sized?"

The giant spider statue was carved out of obsidian, a black volcanic glass. They would have to examine it closer, but from the distance and lit by the liquid torch, the statue looked to be carved out of a single piece of the stone. This raised numerous questions.

Intricately carved.

Calvin and Crawford stepped first, followed by everyone else. The closer they got the more details seemed to emerge from the shrine. Even with its legs bent in a crouch, the spider was impossibly tall. It was difficult to gauge how tall the statue would be at full extension, but it was clearly taller than ten feet. Maybe as tall as fifteen feet. Its total length looked to be close to thirty feet, more than half the length of the entire temple atop the mismatched ziggurat. Each of the eight segmented legs were as thick around as anyone in the party, save for Javier. The legs, however, seemed to be covered in coarse hairs.

"Holy," Del Campo said, and trailed off into silence.

While the others were admiring the legs and slowly moving upward, Professor Gus Del Campo had already turned his gaze up to the head of the beast. Looking down on them with a fierce growl was the head of an enormous jaguar resting atop the giant spider. Its mouth was agape. Its sharp, elongated teeth looked to be carved from diamonds. Its eyes, rubies. It wore a crown that looked to be made of bones – all with precious gems inlaid.

"The Decapitator," Calvin said. "A chief deity of the Moche civilization. Fearsome. Punitive. The headsman. He accepted offerings in the form of military enemies."

"This explains the confusing structure of the temple," Crawford said. "Moche and Incan cultures shared some similarities but also some amazing divergences. This pyramid looks to be a grab-bag from numerous tribes … because it is."

Jenny Renard had stepped forward, past the other academics. She had her camera up, snapping a rapid series of photos. Switching over to video mode, she recorded with one hand and reached out her left to touch the statue. One step away, Dario snapped out of his silent reverence.

"No, chica," he called. "Don't."

Her right foot was already in the air and slowly came down on the pad of stones that ringed the Spider God's statue. As soon as she put her foot down, the stone slid into place. It only moved a half an inch, but she lost her balance – falling backward against Calvin.

The team stood motionless as a series of clunks and thumps seemed to cascade around the outer perimeter of the cavern. It was hard to locate them due to the sheer size of the space and the echoing walls as well as the dramatic angles of the ziggurat itself.

"That's not good," Hart said.

After half a dozen heavy clunks, they heard a new sound. Smaller, but just as ominous. It was a continuous punctuation that seemed to be moving, slowly, toward them.

Click clack. Click clack. Click clack.

Edmundo unholstered his pistol and held it in his left hand while making the sign of the cross with his right.

"This might get bad," Crawford said.

**

The team would split up, it was decided, even though it evoked horror-movie visions. The two students – Calvin and Jenny – would stay on the top of the temple and provide an overwatch with Edmundo. The four soldiers all activated their walkie-talkie communicators so they could stay in contact. Javier and Buzz Crawford went to secure the entrance they came through to first see the ziggurat. Dario, Ramon, Del Campo and Remy Hart went to spy down the two southern tunnels leading away from the temple and cavern.

And then everything fell apart.

SEVEN

Flames continued to lick along the dramatic angles of the ziggurat and the Spider Temple perched atop it. Edmundo shed his backpack and placed it against one of the outer walls of the shrine, the southern wall, as he watched one group make their way around the perimeter of the cavern. Edmundo then held his pistol in one hand and the walkie-talkie in the other.

He began making a circuit around the shrine, watching all sides of the massive hollow mountain for any activity. Edmundo made it all the way back around twice and stopped to watch Dario venture into the mouth of one of the southern tunnels. Cal and Jenny stood next to him and watched them. For now, the ominous click clack click sounds had stopped.

The two soldiers and Professors Del Campo and Hart, holding weapons and powerful flashlights, were nearly ten feet down the cave when a sudden sound startled everyone.

A roar ten times louder than the clicks. And it seemed to come from everywhere at once. Simultaneously, the flames illuminating the ziggurat seemed to explode outward creating an instant, but temporary, six-foot-tall wall of fire straight up in the air.

Edmundo, Jenny and Calvin jumped backward, away from both the sound and the sudden fire. Calvin tripped and fell over one of the shoulder straps of the soldier's backpack. He struggled momentarily to get his bearings. When he did, he popped right back up to his feet. Jenny had watched him and even as he stood, she was looking past him to the floor – the roof of the ziggurat. Almost as soon as they appeared, the flames had died back down to their original height – just barely above the stone channel that contained the dark oil-like substance.

Edmundo keyed his walkie-talkie.

"Overwatch to commander," he said in Spanish and waited for a response.

"Go ahead, Edmundo," came the static-y voice of Dario. "We're fine down here. Just a little rattled." The team of four had just exited the cave and re-entered the giant cavern.

"I think it came from the other south tunnel, boss," Edmundo said into his small communicator.

Dario nodded in agreement even though the gesture was completely swallowed by darkness and shadows before overwatch could actually register it.

"Copy that," Dario said and clipped his walkie-talkie to his belt. He then pulled his pistol back out of the holster, looked at Ramon, and turned to his right to explore the other tunnel. Ramon steeled his nerves, took a breath and followed. Dr. Hart just watched the two soldiers. She had been unnerved by the horrifying roar and the click-clack noise but they had made it all the way through the dense jungle – losing a student along the way – and now had to face whatever new challenges awaited them. She looked at Dr. Del Campo who hefted an eyebrow and gave her a lopsided smile. It was as if he could read her mind. The two professors were carrying machetes while the two soldiers held pistols. Gus shrugged.

"In for a penny," he said, "in for a pound."

**

Javier and Dr. Crawford had taken up position at their main exit from the cavern. The big soldier had stood motionless when the mysterious roar had echoed out into the huge chamber, but the professor had stumbled back a few steps.

"What the hell was that?" he asked his companion.

Javier gripped the machete in one hand and the pistol in the other. He had clipped his walkie talkie to the shoulder strap of his backpack. Against his expansive chest and shoulders, the hand-sized communications device looked like a child's toy.

In response to the question, Javier simply shrugged.

"I do not know," he grumbled as if choosing his words carefully.

From this distance, the ziggurat looked like something out of a video game. With its six torches lit across the façade and the channels of low flames carved into its sharp edges, it looked bizarre against the backdrop of the enormous cavern.

The soldier bent down and placed the machete on the dirt floor at his feet. He shrugged off the backpack and handed the professor a spare pistol from an inner pocket. Crawford took it and nodded.

"Gracias," he said.

"No mas de papa," Javier said and grinned to himself.

**

Jenny had continued looking at the floor past Calvin's legs for several moments after he stood up. By this time, Edmundo had again started making circuits around the outer perimeter of the shrine and he was on the opposite side of the structure.

"What is it?" Cal asked, turning to follow her gaze.

The grad student jumped forward and picked an object up off the ground. It had fallen out of Edmundo's backpack when it was kicked during the ferocious roar. As soon as Calvin saw it, his eyes went wide.

The garish pink protective cover and the circular phone grip with the colorful butterfly on it.

"It's Annika's phone," Jenny said, breathless and wide-eyed. She smoothly slid it into the back of her waistband as Edmundo came back around the corner of the shrine. The two students turned to look at the cavern floor as the group of four made their way to the second tunnel on the south side of the chamber. Edmundo passed the two students and stopped to watch the action – his circuitous route on hold for the moment.

Calvin and Jenny looked at each other. They were peering over the side of the ziggurat six feet away from Edmundo. She quickly took the phone and passed it to Calvin who put it in his thigh pocket. He slowly zipped it closed, careful not to make any sound. Not that it would have mattered. Edmundo was staring intently at his boss and holding his breath as they approached the tunnel.

From their position near the temple, they could just start to see the group on the floor collect themselves to move to the other tunnel. The click clack click rhythm had started up again and began to increase in speed.

**

The small group of four – two soldiers and two academics – made the slow trek from the mouth of one tunnel to the mouth of the other. During this time the click-clack sound sped up and, at the same time, got louder. Suddenly, however, it stopped. Dario and Ramon paused to look at each other. Even though this was a fluid, unknown situation, any significant change could be serious. The unidentified sound was something to be tracked and mapped out.

The eerie silence continued, punctuated only by the flickering of the channel-fires that ringed the giant ziggurat in the center of the cavern. Across the open space, Javier and Crawford stood at the ready, peering into the darkness. Likewise, Edmundo and the two students crouched against the flaming walls of the shrine level of the temple.

Slowly, the team of four continued walking toward the other southern passageway leading away from the stone structure. They proceeded about ten feet into the tunnel, illuminated by the strong beams of their high-powered flashlights and headlamps. Suddenly, they froze in place as another unearthly howl erupted from the darkness. It echoed around them followed by a great whoosh of air. Aided by their military training and practice on the security force, Dario and Ramon dived out of the way. The two academics weren't so well-trained.

Gus Del Campo sensed something was wrong and reacted just a moment too late. He dove sideways to push Hart out of the way of the onrushing evil, but he couldn't get clear himself. They could only see brief flickers of the scene highlighted by the beams of the scattered headlamps and flashlights. It was a spider of gargantuan proportions. Even bigger, if it was possible, than the statue atop the ziggurat. As it rushed at them from the darkness of the tunnel, it swiped its most forward right leg from left to right. It missed the two soldiers who had dived and rolled back toward the tunnel entrance.

It missed Remy Hart who had been knocked down by Del Campo. The thunderous swipe caught Del Campo directly in the chest, however. There was a sickening crack as the man's ribcage caved inward. He might have been dead before the second sickening crack of his head smashing into the stone tunnel wall with incredible force.

With another roar, the great spider crouched and bit down on Del Campo's head – chewing it right off his body.

Dr. Hart screamed.

The spider filled the tunnel, but even more strange was that it had the head of a jaguar, glowing eyes and disproportionately enormous mouth full of razor-sharp teeth. As he chewed on Gus Del Campo's head, he seemed to lean back in pleasure. The click-clack of the ring of bones – a crown that seemed to be constructed of desiccated human bones – atop his head punctuated the movement of his chomping jaws.

Hart and the two soldiers scrambled to their feet and ran from the tunnel.

The enormous spider feasting on Gus's head was perhaps the only thing that saved them from a similar fate. Running at full speed, they made it to the darkened corner of the ziggurat in just over twenty seconds. They stood in the shadows, gasping for air, pressed tightly up against the stone and mud wall of the structure. With another roar, the spider ran out of the tunnel and slid to a halt, startled by the flames lit along the temple structure.

"Madre de Dios," Edmundo breathed before lifting his pistol and sighting down the barrel toward the giant spider. At this range, a handgun was anything but accurate, but the soldier had years of practice and training – so he was confident in hitting the big target. He fired three shots in quick succession. Unfortunately, they all missed and only served to wake the spider out of its semi-trance staring at the fiery beauty of the flaming ziggurat. With another roar, the spider bounded forward.

Blam, blam, blam.

Shots came from the entrance tunnel as Javier also raised his weapon. He was even further away than Edmundo, but knew he had to distract the monster. Unfortunately, his plan worked too well, as the spider made a quick calculation and decided to end the small human who blocked an escape path.

The Spider God wheeled quickly from moving toward the back right corner of the huge ziggurat and screeched in the direction of the incoming shots. It turned and ran at full speed toward the two men standing at the mouth of the tunnel the entire group had entered nearly an hour ago.

For Javier and Crawford, it was something directly out of a nightmare. With the crackle of the fires lining the perimeter of the ziggurat and the long shadows thrown by the channel fire and the numerous torches that lined the front of the structure the spider seemed to grow in fast motion as it galloped toward them.

To his credit, Javier stood his ground and continued firing. Several shots kicked up puffs of dust and dirt as they flew wide of their target and crashed into the ground around the enormous spider. Two, however, hit their mark, directly into the chest of the monster. The spider slowed and staggered to its right but continued moving forward. Eventually, Javier ran dry but continued pulling the trigger. He soon realized that his magazine was empty and threw his gun to the side.

Crawford was frozen in place, mouth gaping open, watching the spider bear down on them.

In other parts of the cavern, Hart, Dario and Ramon sprinted across the open space toward the tunnel from which the spider had emerged. Seeing this, Edmundo called to the two students, Calvin and Jenny, to run downstairs and join them.

"Vamos," Edmundo said and grabbed his backpack off the floor of the temple. "Let's go." They started rushing down the stairs that ringed the ziggurat. Going down, fortunately, was much faster than climbing the structure. As they were going down the stairs, they heard Javier stop firing and looked in that direction as a group.

In the entrance tunnel, Javier had thrown his handgun to the ground and reached behind his back with his left hand. He fumbled for just a second and pulled a grenade out of a hidden pouch on the underside of his backpack. Turning back to look at the huge spider, he pulled the pin and reared back to heave the hunk of metal toward the monster. Unfortunately, the spider lunged forward and swiped a powerful blow downward with its front right leg. Such was the power of the strike, that the spider completely tore Javier's left arm off at the shoulder. After that, three things happened in sequence – but so quickly that they almost happened at the same time.

First, Javier dropped immediately to his knees. The fact that he had lost his arm was almost secondary as he was going into shock based solely on the appearance of the gargantuan spider looming above him. There was a growing puddle of blood mixing with the dirt and creating a mess of disgusting mud. He was almost crouching on the severed arm. The grenade, though, clattered about four feet to his left, coming to rest against the intricately carved wall of the tunnel.

Second, Dr. Crawford saw the grenade and realized what it was. In truth, he hadn't even seen Javier pull it out of his backpack. The professor had been staring at the giant spider, motionless, in utter disbelief. However, the sight of the explosive device shocked him into motion as he turned and ran straight back into the tunnel. He moved quickly away from Javier, the grenade, the spider and the ziggurat. He only got a few lunging steps before his feet got tangled up and he fell to the dusty floor of the ornate cave.

Finally, the spider picked up on all these reactions in a split-second. Its warrior-brain quickly put all the disparate elements together and came to a conclusion – that small object was somehow dangerous. The front man had meant it to harm the Spider God. The man behind ran away from it even lying on the floor – it was clear he was running from the object rather than the spider. Armed with this information, the jaguar-headed monster leapt backward putting a dozen feet between itself and the fallen soldier, Javier, who only now fell to his side on the bloody floor of the tunnel. Whether it was from shock or blood loss or both, the color had drained from his face. Still, he stared at the monster.

The Spider God continued to watch the tunnel even as it stood in the cavern in the shadow of its ziggurat. For a short, silent count, the three combatants stared at each other and then …

BOOM.

The grenade erupted, sandwiched in the corner of the two earthen surfaces. The spider ducked backward from the violent sound even as the tunnel began to cave in on top of the two fallen men. Dust, dirt and other particulate debris billowed into the cavern and enveloped the spider who had risen to its full height. Behind it, Edmundo and the two students ran into the closer southern cavern – the original one Dario had led his team into only five minutes earlier.

The Spider God roared in both anger and confusion. The entrance tunnel was now completely caved in. He slowly turned around to assess the cavern. The ziggurat was ablaze in its fiery lines. The other tiny humans had all disappeared.

**

Three headlamps, three flashlights. Dario, Ramon and Hart ran down the southern cave directly across from the back corner of the ziggurat. Much like the entrance to the cavern, the walls were carved smooth and almost had a polished quality to them. Both the floor and ceiling, however, were rough to the touch yet carved generally flat. Unlike the entrance to the cavern, there were no symbols or carved pictograms of any sort on the walls.

They ran, hoping for an exit or a hiding place from the giant spider. The group turned left then right then left. Ramon had been running forward and frequently turning backward to watch the rear. Dario was in the lead and they had Hart sandwiched between them. After the third turn, they heard a huge explosion that rumbled down the corridor. Dario slid to a halt, momentarily, and looked behind them, around the last corner.

Wordlessly, all three people turned and started running deeper into what was starting to feel like something of a maze. There was one more right turn and then the corridor sharply widened on both sides. Following these gradual angles after just about one hundred feet, the tunnel opened up into a circular room.

Before they got there, however, they noticed the carvings on the corridor walls. What had started as smoothly-polished walls suddenly became crowded with images.

"It's a war," Hart said, slowing enough to look at the wall to her left. She pointed both her headlamp and the powerful beam of the military flashlight at the wall.

The images were moving from the left to the right, telling a story. It was two groups of warriors carrying swords, shields and spears separated by a battlefield. The imagery was stunning in its detail. Hart could even make out different symbols carved into the shields – images on the flying banners. The next huge segment of the image was the actual battle. These warriors clashed on the rolling landscape with a mountain range in the background.

She looked briefly at the other side of the corridor. It was a similar scene in a different environment. One of the armies had the same symbols as the ones on the first wall. Clearly these were the warriors fighting under the Moche banners. In this image, she could almost make out palm trees and a harsh ocean behind them.

Back to the original side of the corridor and the battle progressed. The landscape was littered by dead bodies. Each consecutive segment seemed to have fewer and fewer active warriors. It became clear that the Moche were winning. In the second-to-last segment, the remaining Moche warriors had surrounded their surviving rivals. In the final segment before the corridor opened up into a full-sized room, the remaining Moche had started marching the losing warriors off to the right, essentially, into the room.

This was mirrored almost segment-for-segment on the opposite wall. Just a different landscape. A different enemy.

"Wow," Hart said as she finally joined Dario and Ramon in the room at the end of the corridor.

**

The first thing they noticed was that the room was circular, more than fifty feet across. The walls were rough, but they couldn't make out any detail with their flashlights at that distance. There was a huge stone structure in the center of the chamber. As they slowly approached it, they could see that it was a table, sturdy, with perfect circles drilled out at each corner.

There was also a hole in the center of the slab, leading into a void in the middle of the stone formation. Ramon crouched down to look in. The void was only accessible from one side of the structure.

"For ropes," Dario said, running his fingers across the mouth of one of the holes. He then turned and strode over to the wall. "Oh no," he said.

Hart and Ramon quickly joined him.

It wasn't that the walls were roughly-hewn. There were shelves carved into the walls curving all the way around its circumference. The shelves were stacked with bones. Skulls were the easiest to make out, but there were also ribcages and stacks of smaller femurs, vertebrae and other bones completely ringing the room.

"This is a sacrificial chamber," Hart said, putting all the pieces together. "Ropes through the holes on the slab to hold the victim down. Drainage. The bones." She paused again and looked back at the table. "Torture and sacrifice."

Then, they all looked toward the corridor they had entered from. The gentle sounds of click clack click echoed off the rock walls.

**

The only way in or out of the room was the corridor they had originally come from. The corridor that started narrow and gently widened while showing the detail of two Moche battles. Whether the battles were real or fictitious, accurate or exaggerated, they would have to research it later

– comparing the landscape, symbols, armor. Remy Hart, in the back of her head, planned to take as many photos as possible of all the battle segments to match them up with any historical records.

But first, they would have to deal with the Spider God.

Click clack click.

The sounds were not speeding up, but they seemed to be getting closer. The echoes continued to slide their way down the twisting and turning corridor just outside the torture room. The team of three was arranged around the stone altar in the center of the circular room. They all faced the wide entry, weapons at the ready.

Click clack click.

And then silence. Hart took three long, slow breaths and still nothing happened. There were no additional sounds until, with a screech, the giant spider rounded the final corner of the corridor and hurtled itself down the ornate path. Half down the tunnel, the spider roared. It was deafening and echoed around the circular chamber as if the structure was built to contain and amplify the sound. The three team members were momentarily stunned to the point that no one fired their weapon until the enormous spider was actually inside the room.

The spider made a jagged jump to its right, to the left of the stone table. It swung a giant right leg, as thick as a grown man's torso, and caught Ramon on the side of the head. The force of the blow propelled Ramon's head sideways and downward until it smashed against the surface of the stone altar with a sickening thump. In an involuntary reaction, Dr. Hart screamed. At the same time, Dario dived to his side completely under the height of the altar. The spider turned from Ramon and faced Hart. It crouched to look at her with its huge jaguar mouth open, teeth gleaming in the light of her headlamp. As she continued screaming, the spider sucked in a deep breath and roared back at her.

And simply bit her head off.

Dr. Hart's decapitated body crumpled, overtaken by gravity and slack muscles. The spider, thoughtfully, chewed through the head. The sounds of the skull splintering were muffled but still audible as Dario struggled to reload his pistol. He had crawled around the corner of the altar – putting the stone structure between himself and the spider. In fact, Dario was nearest the corridor entrance. He briefly thought about making a break for it. As soon as the thought registered, however, it was quickly dismissed. There was no way he could make it all the way back down the twisty path faster than the gigantic spider. And even if he did reach the mouth of the cave, where would he go? The temple? The other corridor?

He racked a live chamber into his weapon and spun to face the spider. Dario knew the only way would be to kill the beast. He would have to put as many bullets into the brain of the grotesque jaguar head until it …

Crack.

The Spider God climbed fully over the stone altar and stepped on Dario with its two huge front legs. Unfortunately, the soldier was half standing against the structure and the spider bent the man's spine in a spot it wasn't meant to be bent. Dario's torso was bent in half, the bones of his ribcage piercing nearly every internal organ at the same time. The soldier's mouth hung slack as he slid from the edge of the altar and crumpled on the floor.

The spider roared in triumph and then looked around at the three dead bodies in what used to be the room dedicated to its glory. There were other humans in the temple, but first, a snack.

**

Three headlamps, three flashlights. Edmundo, Calvin and Jenny ran down the other southern cave directly across from the bottom of the stairs at the front corner of the ziggurat. They didn't see the other team of three enter the nearby tunnel. But they did have a front-row view of the explosion in the entrance corridor. They covered the distance quickly – while the cave-in was happening. Well before the giant spider turned around from the action it was directly involved in.

Much like the entrance to the cavern, the walls were carved smooth and almost had a polished quality to them. Both the floor and ceiling, however, were rough to the touch yet carved generally flat. Unlike the entrance to the cavern, there were no symbols or carved pictograms of any sort on the walls.

The group turned right, left and another right as they ran down the twisting tunnels. As they made another left, the team started slowing just a bit. There were three things strange about this section of the corridor. First, it seemed to be widening at a gradual clip. If the end of the tunnel they had just entered was ten feet across, it looked like the opposite end was about twice that width.

Second, the walls were decorated again, similar to the main entrance. There were carvings on both sides of the widening corridor. They were different carvings but seemed to tell similar stories. They were stories of construction.

"Is this," Jenny said, shining both her flashlight and headlamp at one image out of dozens, "is this our mountain?"

Calvin leaned in and was also looking at the carving. It did, indeed, look like Little Sister Mountain. In fact, it looked like the view he had seen in his hallucination. It was before the mining village but after the small path to the cave entrance on the right side.

"Sure looks like it," Cal said.

"Vamos, vamos," Edmundo said. "We need to move." He had continued moving down the tunnel, undeterred by the ornate, detailed carvings. He was now two-thirds of the way down the corridor, looking back at the final turn, worried that the spider would catch up to them. He wasn't sure where this tunnel led, but the hope was that it would be some sort of secret escape. Possibly, all four of the tunnels around the ziggurat would somehow lead out of the mountain … much like the fifth corridor, the one they entered from, led to the cave and path to the river.

Cal and Jenny started moving again, but slowly.

"I think it's the story of them building the ziggurat," she said.

The carvings along the left side of the corridor were broken up into twelve panels. There weren't hard borders, but the images were arranged in such a way to indicate twelve separate parts to the story. The initial image, the establishing shot, as they said in Mr. Conway's "Screenwriting 101" class, was of the peak of Little Sister. The next was a detailed carving of the hollow mountain. Pre-ziggurat. There were several workers in the carving if for no other reason than to give the negative space a dramatic sense of size. The artisan had also represented shafts of light cascading down from the cavern's roof.

The next panel showed an army of workers constructing the first floor of the enormous ziggurat. Now half down the corridor, Calvin turned and shone his lights against the opposite side of the polished cave corridor. These were gruesome accounts of the Spider God's conquests. There were heroic images across all twelve panels. In some, the giant spider was fighting a huge army. In others, it was fighting what appeared to be other gods – a huge crocodile, a giant eagle, and so on. On the final panel as the corridor continued widening was a somewhat serene scene. It was the Spider God in a huge circular room with a large stone pedestal in the center. There were no people in the room. The spider seemed to be crouched, gazing at the empty table as if waiting for something.

"A sacrificial chamber," Calvin said. "Great."

The third thing that was strange about the corridor, though, was overtaken by the carved panels, but it was just as odd. After spending so many steps of the tunnel in darkness, the flaming liquid seemed to make its way into this space as well. It lined the left side of the corridor where the floor met the carved wall. It ran the length of the corridor and led them into the next room.

A huge circular room like the final panel.

**

Instead of a stone altar, however, the center of the circular room was a smaller version of the shrine that stood atop the enormous ziggurat in the hollow mountain. Unlike the large shrine, however, the place of honor in this smaller version was not a life-sized statue of the spider, but a ten-foot-tall monolith. It was carved from the same obsidian as the spider, but it was a symbol rather than a portrait. It looked like the Egyptian Ankh – the representation for eternal life. It looked like a capital letter T with an elongated head resting atop. In this statue, however, the bulbous head seemed to be on fire and each of the three stems were covered in deadly-sharp spikes. None of the team members touched them for fear of pain or poison.

They were getting a clear look at the shrine, though, as the flaming liquid had flowed along the channel from the corridor, into the room, and encircled the temple much like it did in the big ziggurat. In this room, the flames stretched nearly a foot out of the top of the small chambers.

Arranged in a circle around the statue were six smaller statues in different materials. There was the spider, only two feet tall, carved out of the same obsidian. There was a gold crocodile. A marble snake. A jade eagle. The final two – one in silver and one in ruby – were animals none of the team recognized.

"Strange," Jenny said, keying in on the two mystery portraits. "Extinct species?"

Calvin shrugged.

Edmundo had continued past the small temple and found another small doorway.

"Move," he said, stepping through. He stopped after only a few steps.

"Oh no," Jenny said. There was no exit. This room was a dead end.

**

It was a circular room with beds lining the walls. Twelve beds in total. They were arranged like bunk beds … with an upper and lower sleeping area. Calvin stepped up close to one of the beds – he held his flashlight up high, as the flaming chambers did not continue into this room.

It was a skeleton. They were all skeletons. All twelve beds each contained a skeleton.

"Oh my God," Jenny said, covering her mouth with the non-flashlight hand.

"We're trapped," Cal said, looking around the room.

Edmundo had seemed to already come to this conclusion. He no longer had the frenzied look on his face from moments ago, but now simply looked defeated. He had stepped toward the bed closest to him at the back of the circular chamber.

"These were holy men," he said, reaching into the bed and pulling out what looked like a thick, gold, ornamental necklace. It was jewel-encrusted and certainly denoted a position of status. There was a small carving of a spider, again in obsidian, set against a huge circular gold medallion at the base of the necklace. "Perhaps keepers of the temples. The ziggurat. They don't look mauled in any way. Perhaps they died peacefully."

Absently, he folded the necklace into one of his pockets. Suddenly, they heard screaming and gunfire.

"What the…" Cal said, stepping away from the wall.

The sounds were muffled and sounded like they had carried a great distance through the rock, but that could have only been an acoustic trick. Numerous shots rang out and they could hear a high-pitched scream that might have been Professor Hart.

Then, suddenly, everything went quiet again.

**

They frantically looked around for an exit. A secret door. A hidden passage. A covered path such as the path into the cavern. Nothing became readily apparent. Passing a skeleton, Cal grabbed one of the desiccated legs of a dead holy man. It was the femur, the thigh bone, and one of the strongest bones of the body. Nearly two feet long, the femur was dry and hard as a rock. Unfortunately, Cal worried that it was also brittle, having rested here undisturbed for a hundred years. Panicked, Jenny grabbed the other femur from the same bed. For his part, Edmundo steadied himself against the far wall, opposite the door. He was at a slight angle and could see a little past the flaming shrine into the large corridor. From this perspective, the corridor seemed to be shrinking in width – narrowing until it disappeared around a corner.

Click clack click.

The subtle yet horrifying sound echoed down the twists and turns of the chamber. Calvin armed a sheen of sweat off his face in one smooth move from his forehead to under his chin. Jenny was trembling violently and gripping the femur so hard her knuckles screamed out in pain. These two had taken up position on the left of the door – from the perspective of the shrine – with Edmundo behind them.

Click clack click.

The sound did not speed up in its rhythm, but it somehow got louder. The three remaining adventurers knew the Spider God had them trapped. As soon as the priests' room dead ended, they knew their fates were sealed even if they didn't discuss it out loud.

Click clack.

The sound stopped and the final 'clack' echoed down the widening chamber. Calvin gripped the femur like a baseball bat. He held his breath. He stood in front of Jenny and peered round the corner of the doorway out to the temple. Suddenly, a great roar erupted from beyond the final turn of the tunnel and crashed its way down the spider carvings into the shrine. The flames around the small temple exploded upward, more than doubling in height until the echoes of the spider's roar died down. He had pulled his head back in shock at the sudden eruption.

"I think I have an idea," he whispered to Jenny.

"What?"

"Follow my lead," he said.

Unfortunately, through this, he didn't see the giant spider erupt from around the corner and bound toward them into the shrine room.

The spider paused a moment and glanced at the temple erected in his honor – and the honor of its sibling deities. The head of the spider-jaguar slowly turned as it took in the entirety of the room. After making a turn, it saw through the door into the resting chamber with Edmundo standing against the wall. The Spider God recognized the weapon in his hands, but also saw the gold necklace – spider medallion visible – hanging out of the soldier's pocket.

The spider crouched and burst through the door into the holy room toward the final soldier.

Edmundo, for his part, started screaming and firing his weapon at the onrushing monster. His aim was true, though, unlike his counterparts, and several shots found their way into the body of the beast. One shot tore through the left side of the jaguar's face, ruining the jaw hinge on that side. With a shriek, the spider pounced forward.

Moments earlier, when the spider had crossed the threshold of the resting chamber, Cal and Jenny quickly stepped out of the room and stood by the small Ankh shrine. They stood on opposite ends of the temple and waited.

The soldier fired his weapon empty. And, while the spider was seriously wounded, it kept coming. It knocked Edmundo down with a crushing blow from high-left to low-right with a powerful left leg. Edmundo crumpled to the ground, his neck broken. With is eyes wide in terror, the soldier could do little more than twitch in agony as the Spider God began to rhythmically trample his face and head.

**

Watching from the shrine room, Calvin saw this and dry-heaved as Edmundo's head became little more than a dark spot in the dirt at the back of the chamber. It looked like a thin puddle of raspberry jam.

Cal heaved again and his breath caught in his throat.

The Spider God turned slowly, moving only its head. It heaved and sucked wind through its ruined mouth. It had never been this wounded and the pain and anger had somehow melded together into a white-hot hatred of the two humans standing next to its temple. Fully turned inside the holy rest chamber, the spider did not recognize the same type of weapons the soldiers had used. It saw the clubs held low by the two tiny humans. It looked first right then left, the blood pouring from its shattered face. It was almost looking upon the resting forms of the dead holy men for some guidance, approval or insight. Human to human. Subservient to subservient. The bones were silent. With a half-roar that caused more pain than fear in those around it, the giant beast began slowly walking into the shrine room.

Quickly calculating the distance, as he had seen the spider explode in movement, Calvin crouched a bit lower into his stance.

"Watch," he hissed at Jenny who stared through the open temple structure at the other student. "Like Dario did."

Calvin lowered his stance even more and reached behind him with the femur. He dipped it into the fire, held it for a second and then quickly swept it forward like he was rowing a boat through choppy water in reverse. The movement caused a rainbow arc of flaming, viscous liquid to streak through the air, catching the spider in the chest and face. The heavy liquid stuck to the spider's skin and the coarse hair that covered its body. Jenny, seeing the strategy, did the same with her femur on her side of the temple. Soon, the spider's thorax was a flaming, blistering mess.

The Spider God howled in pain. It lurched forward and swung its right front leg at Calvin who ducked out of the way. The student rolled backward and quickly splashed another jet of fire at the monster. Jenny had cautiously moved to the perpendicular side of the temple and swept her second line of fire at the beast's side. It stumbled away from the fire, crouching down on its four front legs.

Calvin, again dipped into the fire and threw one more arc of flames at the spider – which caught it directly in the face. The Spider God screeched in horror and fully dropped to the floor. The air in the room was heavy with burning hair and bubbling flesh. Cal looked at the femur and it was a flaming wreck as parts of it began crumbling away. Jenny, from her position at the back of the temple, hurled one more load of flaming liquid at the collapsed spider. In perfect, accidental, timing she lost her grip on the femur and it flew the ten feet from her spot to the side of the spider. The flaming, splintered thigh-bone launched through the air and punctured the side of the beast, lighting its internal organs on goopy fire.

With a final cry of pain, the Spider God died on the floor of a temple erected in its honor, mere feet from a chamber where countless souls expired in its name.

Calvin and Jenny backed away and watched from the expanded corridor entrance at the front of the shrine room. They watched the spider's breathing slow, finally, to a stop.

"Shit," Calvin said and smiled at Jenny.

EPILOGUE

Cal and Jenny spent much of the next hour wandering around the caverns collecting supplies from their dead compatriots. They had to stop several times to vomit at the disgusting displays. They brought numerous backpacks, flashlights and weapons to the top of the ziggurat.

They had clicked off all the lights save for a headlamp each and started stacking their remaining food and supplies near the base of the huge temple atop the hidden ziggurat. The two graduate students had planned to organize everything and take an inventory before starting to search the other two corridors to see if they could find some sort of escape hatch. Another way out of the hollow mountain of Little Sister.

Still illuminated by the flaming channels of thick liquid, they sat down for a quick rest before the next step of their journey.

"You know, people believe the Great Sphinx of Giza in Egypt was crafted about 4,500 years ago during the time of the Pharoah Khafre," Calvin said, sitting and leaning his head against the stone wall of the ziggurat.

"Uh huh."

"There's a fringe theory, though, that suggests the structure is thousands of years older," he continued. "Built something like 12,000 years ago. They cite the horizontal levels of erosion and other factors. Like that the patterns of weather damage don't line up with other structures of similar ages."

"Plus the head," Jenny shrugged.

Calvin smiled.

"Yes. Plus the head. The head of the Sphinx is way too small compared to its body. The ancient Egyptians were incredible observers of nature and the body. There's no way they would carve such a magnificent structure that was so horribly out of proportion. Some theorists have suggested that it was the head of a lion originally, or even Anubis, and was re-carved in the likeness of Khafre after erosion had damaged the original head beyond repair."

They were silent for a moment. The crackle and hiss of flames punctuated the stillness.

"The point is that we don't know. We can make theories until we're blue in the face. But without any kind of actual historical record, we just don't know. The Great Sphinx was obviously there first, and the pyramids were built around it. What if the Sphinx was the centerpiece of a super-ancient civilization of which we have lost all records? *Ancient* ancient Egyptians? We could probably research those carvings we saw on the two corridors. Heck, there might be carvings on every corridor. We know there were carvings on the entrance. We might be able to piece together the construction of this temple. Maybe. Maybe not. What if this mountain was hollowed out a million years ago?"

Pensive for a moment, Calvin leaned his head back again. He took a bite from a protein snack bar. And rationed a sip of water.

He swallowed and took a deep breath to start speaking again but something distracted him. A sound where there should be none. It was the small rumble of a heavy stone rolling and coming to rest on the ground. Jenny and Cal stood up and looked around the cavern. They each grabbed a flashlight and peered into the eerie flickering darkness of the hollow mountain peak.

Another small rumble.

It was Jenny who located it and pointed.

"The entrance," she said.

They both picked up salvaged weapons, reloaded from the soldiers' stash and quickly made their way down the ninety-one and a half steps of the massive ziggurat. They jogged toward the entrance tunnel, weapons and flashlights held at the ready.

There was another small rumble and they could actually see the movement that caused it. A huge stone rolled from the caved-in tunnel into the cavern. They both slid to a halt at the mouth of the cavern entrance as a hand punched through the dirt. Cal and Jenny quickly dropped their gear and rushed forward to pull dirt and rocks away from the hand.

"Professor," Calvin yelled as Crawford pushed his face through the collapsed tunnel into the huge void.

"Sweet baby Jesus," Crawford said as he slid down the small hill. "Calvin. Jenny." He looked around to see if there were any others in the cavern. "The spider?"

Calvin shook his head.

"Jenny killed it," he said and smiled. "Unfortunately, we're all that's left."

Crawford slowly nodded his head.

"Javier didn't make it," he said. "He took the brunt of both the explosion and the cave in. I was far enough away to make it out of the danger zone. Tried to dig my way back to you all. It seems as if I missed all the fun."

Calvin and Jenny sat down on either side of the dirty, sweaty professor of religious theory.

"You and I have very different definitions of fun," Cal said. "Our escorts were all carrying small campsite shovels. How about we have some dinner and start digging our way outta here?"

"Capital idea," Crawford said.

He stood up, brushed the dirt from his thighs and smiled when he realized it did no good.

"I'm parched," he said, walking off toward the cavern temple.

THE END

STEVE METCALF has explored writing short fiction, novellas, novels, feature length screenplays and screenplay shorts. Rather than sticking to one path of style or genre, he simply follows his muse and writes whatever inspires him. From a book about the history of the video game industry to zombies rushing forth from an abandoned gold rush mine, nothing is off limits.

Steve enjoys writing both standalone stories and multi-book tales. The "Objekt 221" science fiction series features countless battles between time-traveling soldiers and Cretaceous dinosaurs. The KPI series centers on the King Paranormal Investigations reality TV crew as they film the fourth season of their popular television show. Further, Steve acts as both project manager and contributor to The Event short story collection each year.

You can interact with the author at
www.steve-metcalf.com

Check out other great

Cryptid Novels!

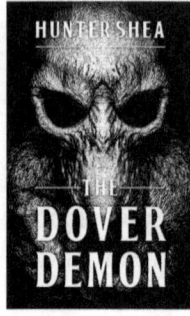

Hunter Shea

THE DOVER DEMON

The Dover Demon is real...and it has returned. In 1977, Sam Brogna and his friends came upon a terrifying, alien creature on a deserted country road. What they witnessed was so bizarre, so chilling, they swore their silence. But their lives were changed forever. Decades later, the town of Dover has been hit by a massive blizzard. Sam's son, Nicky, is drawn to search for the infamous cryptid, only to disappear into the bowels of a secret underground lair. The Dover Demon is far deadlier than anyone could have believed. And there are many of them. Can Sam and his reunited friends rescue Nicky and battle a race of creatures so powerful, so sinister, that history itself has been shaped by their secretive presence? "THE DOVER DEMON is Shea's most delightful and insidiously terrifying monster yet." – Shotgun Logic Reviews "An excellent horror novel and a strong standout in the UFO and cryptid subgenres." –Hellnotes "Non-stop action awaits those brave enough to dive into the small town of Dover, and if you're lucky, you won't see the Demon himself!" – The Scary Reviews PRAISE FOR SWAMP MONSTER MASSACRE "B-horror movie fans rejoice, Hunter Shea is here to bring you the ultimate tale of terror!" – Horror Novel Reviews "A nonstop thrill ride! I couldn't put this book down." – Cedar Hollow Horror Reviews

Armand Rosamilia

THE BEAST

The end of summer, 1986. With only a few days left until the new school year, twins Jeremy and Jack Schaffer are on very different paths. Jeremy is the geek, playing Dungeons & Dragons with friends Kathleen and Randy, while Jack is the jock, getting into trouble with his buddies. And then everything changes when neighbor Mister Higgins is killed by a wild animal in his yard. Was it a bear? There's something big lurking in the woods behind their New Jersey home.Will the police be able to solve the murder before more Middletown residents are ripped apart?

Check out other great

Cryptid Novels!

Hunter Shea

LOCH NESS REVENGE

Deep in the murky waters of Loch Ness, the creature known as Nessie has returned. Twins Natalie and Austin McQueen watched in horror as their parents were devoured by the world's most infamous lake monster. Two decades later, it's their turn to hunt the legend. But what lurks in the Loch is not what they expected. Nessie is devouring everything in and around the Loch, and it's not alone. Hell has come to the Scottish Highlands. In a fierce battle between man and monster, the world may never be the same. Praise for THEY RISE : "Outrageous, balls to the wall...made me yearn for 3D glasses and a tub of popcorn, extra butter!" – The Eyes of Madness "A fast-paced, gore-heavy splatter fest of sharksploitation." The Werd "A rocket paced horror story. I enjoyed the hell out of this book." Shotgun Logic Reviews

C.G. Mosley

BAKER COUNTY
BIGFOOT CHRONICLE

Marie Bledsoe only wants her missing brother Kurt back. She'll stop at nothing to make it happen and, with the help of Kurt's friend Tony, along with Sheriff Ray Cochran, Marie embarks on a terrifying journey deep into the belly of the mysterious Walker Laboratory to find him. However, what she and her companions find lurking in the laboratory basement is beyond comprehension. There are cryptids from the forest being held captive there and something...else. Enjoy this suspenseful tale from the mind of C.G. Mosley, author of Wood Ape. Welcome back to Baker County, a place where monsters do lurk in the night!

Check out other great

Cryptid Novels!

Ian Faulkner

CRYPTID

Be careful what you look for. You might just find it.1996. A group of 14 students walked into the trackless virgin forests of Graham Island, British Columbia for a three-day hike. They were never seen again. 2019. An American TV crew retrace those students' steps to attempt to solve a 23-year-old mystery.A disparate collection of characters arrives on the island. But all is not as it seems. Two of them carry dark secrets. Terrible knowledge that will mean death for some – but a fighting chance of survival for others. In the hidden depths of the forests – man is on the menu. Some mysteries should remain unsolved...

Eric S. Brown

LOCH NESS HORROR

The Order of the Eternal Light, a secret organization have foretold the end of the human race. In order to save all humanity, agents of the Order must locate the Loch Ness Monster and obtain a sample of its blood for within in it is the key to stopping the apocalypse but finding the monster will be no easy task.